D0960787

BLOODTRAITOR

BOOKS BY AMELIA ATWATER-RHODES

DEN OF SHADOWS
In the Forests of the Night
Demon in My View
Shattered Mirror
Midnight Predator
Persistence of Memory
Token of Darkness
All Just Glass
Poison Tree
Promises to Keep

THE KIESHA'RA
Hawksong
Snakecharm
Falcondance
Wolfcry
Wyvernhail

THE MAEVE'RA TRILOGY
Bloodwitch
Bloodkin
Bloodtraitor

AMELIA ATWATER-RHODES

BLOODTRAITOR

THE MAEVE'RA
VOLUME III

DELACORTE PRESS

Text copyright © 2016 by Amelia Atwater-Rhodes
Jacket art copyright © 2016 by Sammy Yuen

All rights reserved. Published in the United States by Delacorte Press, an imprint of Random House Children's Books, a division of Penguin Random House LLC, New York.

Delacorte Press is a registered trademark and the colophon is a trademark of Penguin Random House LLC.

Visit us on the Web! randomhouseteens.com

Educators and librarians, for a variety of teaching tools, visit us at RHTeachersLibrarians.com

Library of Congress Cataloging-in-Publication Data
Names: Atwater-Rhodes, Amelia.
Title: Bloodtraitor / Amelia Atwater-Rhodes.
Description: First Edition. | New York : Delacorte Press, [2016] | Series: The Maeve'ra ; volume 3 | Summary: "When a mercenary from the vampires' inner circle proposes a daring plan to bring down the empire of Midnight, Malachi must feign support for his unstable sister so his prophecy can be fulfilled. He must do it for his family, for his people—and for their freedom"—Provided by publisher.
Identifiers: LCCN 2015023325 | ISBN 978-0-385-74307-5 (hardback) | ISBN 978-0-307-98077-9 (ebook)
Subjects: | CYAC: Fantasy. | Shapeshifting—Fiction. | Vampires—Fiction. | Prophecies—Fiction. | Brothers and sisters—Fiction. | BISAC: JUVENILE FICTION / Fantasy & Magic. | JUVENILE FICTION / Legends, Myths, Fables / General. | JUVENILE FICTION / Action & Adventure / Survival Stories.
Classification: LCC PZ7.A8925 Bk 2016 | DDC [Fic]—dc23

The text of this book is set in 12-point Loire.
Jacket design and interior design by Jinna Shin

Printed in the United States of America
10 9 8 7 6 5 4 3 2 1
First Edition

Bloodtraitor is dedicated to Brittany Maresh, a dear friend of mine whose writing, perseverance, dedication, and brilliance are a constant inspiration to me. I couldn't have made it through Maeve'ra without you.

This has been a year of major changes—some wonderful, some horrific, and some still to be decided. I've lost people I never thought I could do without, rediscovered friends I thought gone forever, and learned the incredible love a mother feels for her newborn child. For that reason, *Bloodtraitor* is also dedicated to all the people who come and go in our lives:

To the stranger we speak with for a few minutes on the train, and never see again. To brothers and sisters who stand by us no matter what. To college friends we cherish for a semester and then drift from when the summer comes. To lifelong friends who are as dear to us as family. To Internet buddies and neighborhood pals.

To the people we can't stand, who irritate us, challenge us, frustrate us, and drive us to compete. To the people we admire, who inspire us, encourage us, and push us to achieve. To the cute barista we smile at without asking his or her name, the adolescent crush who broke our heart, and the love of our life. To our teachers—good, bad, and indifferent—and our students. To our bosses, employees, customers, and clients.

Maeve'ra is dedicated to all of you.

PROLOGUE

MACHIAVELLI BELIEVED THAT *the ends justify the means.*

He had many opinions, mostly about what it means to be a leader, and how to maintain peace—and, more importantly, control. He says that it is best for a prince to be both feared and loved, but that if you cannot manage both, it is better to be feared than loved.

A ruler should not be overly generous, except when he can spend that which belongs to others. He should always keep his word, or at least always seem to. He must control his own army through cruelty, because that is the only way to keep his troops' respect, but he should never abuse his subjects so much that they revile him.

I know for a fact that Jeshickah has a copy of Machiavelli's The Prince *on a shelf in her room. I have read it dozens of* times, and I see much of the Italian's philosophy reflected in the vampires' empire.

Midnight's laws are inviolate. The vampires are held to them as strongly as the shapeshifters and witches Midnight rules. A verbal agreement with one of Midnight's leaders or mercenaries is as strong as one etched in stone.

Midnight's conquered lands are allowed to keep their monarchs, their religion, and their culture, but all of those leaders are forced to adhere to Midnight's laws. These puppet kings and queens cannot guarantee their people safety or freedom without Jeshickah's blessing. Only she is powerful and generous enough to give them sovereignty over their own flesh and spirit.

Midnight's laws offer all loyal subjects the coveted title of freeblood. A freeblood man or woman cannot be claimed as a slave, nor can any of his property be seized by the vampires. A shapeshifter can only lose his freeblood status if he violates Midnight's laws, or if he is sold into Midnight by one of his own kind. In that case, it is not by the vampires' will that he loses his freedom, but through the cruelty of his own.

This is a simple way to weaken the loyalty shapeshifters have to their own kind, while avoiding the kind of contempt that Machiavelli warned would give rise to conspirators and the end of a kingdom.

In addition to this generous gift of freedom, Midnight offers beautiful things, which the Diente of the serpiente or the Tuuli Thea of the avians could never hope to match. It provides luxurious markets and maintains trade roads, supporting a global economy in exchange for "reasonable" taxes . . . and the complete reliance on the vampires' continued goodwill.

What of those who refuse to bend to Midnight's law? Those who stand up against it, and cry out, We do not need you! Those who would spit in the face of any king who claimed to "protect" us by allowing the vampires to maintain their sovereignty?

We are branded exiles and traitors, forced to live outside the lines of easy answers and simple definitions of right and wrong.

Diente Julian Cobriana, king of the serpiente, sold my sister and brother into slavery to pay his taxes. I accepted a devil's deal and was able to rescue one of them. Just one.

I left my brother, Shkei, to die in a trainer's cell, not realizing that it was already too late to save anyone. The woman who returned to us looked like my sister, Misha, but she was riddled with madness, and every step she has taken since her return has led us further down a path so dark it is hard to imagine any escape.

Perhaps I have no right to complain about anyone else's clarity of mind, or lack thereof. My falcon blood has kept me teetering on the edge between sanity and utter lunacy all my life. It has infected my days and nights with visions, usually of the darkest moments in my own and others' lives, and made it a daily struggle to remain in the real world with those I still call kin. That weakness almost cost me my life, since Jeshickah saw no use for me.

A serpiente outlaw named Farrell saved my life, and

taught me how to survive and—more importantly—how to love. Now he is gone, just like my brother, just like my sister might as well be, and in the end I cannot help believing that it is my fault.

Malachi Obsidian
June 1804

CHAPTER 1

WAS IT FEAR *that continually brought him back to this place? Loneliness? Desperation?*

Malachi paused in the middle of scrubbing the smooth marble cell floor. The copper tang of blood mingled with the acidic tang of vinegar in his nose, caustic but soothingly familiar. These were the first scents he recalled from his childhood, a combination of abuse and antiseptic, but it wasn't nostalgia that brought him back to Midnight again and again.

Guilt, *his mind whispered to him.* That's what brings you here. You know that, no matter what you say or do, this is where you were made and this is where you belong.

He shook himself, trying to clear the nagging, gnawing thoughts. The watered-down blood on the white marble swirled in his vision, becoming the red bands of a midsummer sunset.

He flattened his wet hands on the smooth stone, trying to force his magic back and keep his awareness in the here and now, but then he clearly heard Farrell's voice saying, "Guards. Too many to fight. Run!"

Malachi's head whipped toward a vision of the man who was the closest thing he had ever had to a father. Farrell had just put himself between a serpiente soldier and Shkei, Malachi's younger brother. Nearby, Aika was standing against two palace guards, wearing a feral grin as she spun the blade-tipped stave she favored as a weapon. Shkei managed to extricate himself, and then they all turned to run.

If Malachi were there, he could have called on his power to help hide his kin as they fled, but even by flight he was hours away. He could only watch.

"You're in the way, Malachi." The vision wavered as strong hands casually pushed him aside. He fell, and the odor of blood overwhelmed him. Was it only here, or was it in his vision, too? Who was hurt?

He shoved himself up on hands and knees and scrambled out of the cell. He needed to get back–

"Malachi!" Frantic, desperate pleas whispered my name. Where was I? *When?* "The guards are gone," the same voice said.

Guards. In the woods. But I was in Midnight—

No, I could smell the forest. Had I made it back to camp?

6

I opened my eyes, and the face leaning over mine slowly became recognizable: slender Vance, the quetzal with emerald- and ruby-colored feathers beneath the chestnut hair that fell around his russet-dark face. His second form was a small, brightly colored bird better suited to its native tropical lands than it was to this cold, rainy place. Seeing him helped me snap back to the present, because that vision was of something that had happened a year ago, and I hadn't known Vance yet then.

Like me, Vance had been born in the heart of the empire known as Midnight. Mindful of the fact that a quetzal cannot survive in captivity, the lords of that realm had kept him in a beautiful greenhouse filled with every luxury, in the hope that he would never realize he was a slave.

After he had escaped that box, they had put him in a larger one. They had showed him the human slaves and the shapeshifter traitors, and had told him, *This is the way the world works.* They had offered him power. I was the one who had shown him the truth . . . as well as I could, anyway. My understanding was obviously flawed, but the terrible day when my siblings had been taken by serpiente guards had taught me one lesson well: there was nothing good to be gained inside Midnight's walls, and too much that could be lost.

Fear of what he could become had driven Vance to the Obsidian guild. To me. To death, probably.

I looked around, trying to get my bearings quickly enough that Vance wouldn't realize how lost I had been in a different time and place. I was a victim of my own power less often these days than I had been when I was a child, but stress, fear, and exhaustion could still combine to overwhelm me.

We were lying on bare earth in the middle of a grove of white birch trees. Two more of our guild huddled with us. Kadee, gentle Kadee with romantic notions and a love of books she could not read and history she could hardly remember, had her knees curled against her chest and was shivering as she tried to keep warm despite the spring chill and pervasive dampness, hanks of sandy-brown hair dripping lankly around her face. Nearest to the edge of the grove was Aika. Scarred and lean and blank-faced, she grasped a weathered, beaten stave with a glistening steel blade at the tip. She must have washed the mud and blood away before I woke.

The guards are gone.

The events of the previous night returned to me like a crashing wave, and I had to bite back an involuntary cry of pain. I remembered the guards streaming into our camp. The ones who had descended upon my guild nearly a year ago had been simple soldiers intent on capturing our people alive. The ones who had assaulted us the night before had been elite royal guards with orders to kill.

Farrell. I remembered seeing him fall. Farrell Obsidian had been our guiding star, the man who had founded our guild. More importantly, he was the one who had rescued me from Midnight when I was seven years old and would have been put down as a worthless failure. He had given me back the voice my volatile magic had stolen from me. Now he was dead.

My fault.

"The guards are gone," Vance repeated, as if I might not have heard him the first time.

I nodded this time, finally acknowledging him, and once more looked around, only to realize that the others were all looking at me, waiting for my next words. The Obsidian guild had no king, no true leader, but these three were allowing me to guide them because Farrell had always trusted me.

Years ago, I had spoken a prophecy: *Someday, my sister, you will be queen. When you and your king rule, you will bow to no one. And this place, this Midnight, will burn to ash.* Farrell Obsidian had known a falcon's gift for prophecy, and so he heeded my statement even though I was just a child. He had bought my freedom, and that of my unborn sister, Misha, and my white-viper mother.

Farrell's mate, Melissa, had never forgiven him for rescuing me, a mostly mad, mute, half-falcon slave from Midnight. She knew that falcons and white vipers both possessed dark magic; she didn't trust me, and had been convinced that my presence would only bring trouble. She had left Farrell, and their son, Aaron, had ended up being raised by the serpiente king.

"Do we have . . . any kind of plan?" Kadee prompted me, when my silence had stretched too long. Though she was only fifteen, Kadee always had a mature quality about her, as if she gave more thought to what she said than most people did. Maybe it came from her human upbringing, or from the way she had been so isolated through the months of terror and pain associated with coming of age as a human-born serpent.

"I don't know," I said. I looked toward where the serpiente guards had camped the night before, remembering how close we had all come to being killed. My magic had hidden the four of us. I didn't know how many others had survived the night.

Before the guards had chased us apart, our guild had been fighting among ourselves. My sister, Misha, had unveiled her plan to ascend to the serpiente throne after selling the current heir, Hara Cobriana, into slavery in Midnight. I had objected, but many of my kin had agreed. I hoped now that most of them had run in the opposite direction, following Misha instead of me. Her intentions disgusted me, but I would rather know that my kin had chosen to follow a path I disapproved of than that they had all been slaughtered.

"We need to warn Hara." Vance grimaced, as if not liking his own words. "Carefully. I don't imagine she will welcome us gratefully if we go speak to her, even if we are trying to protect her." Our guild had been hunted outlaws, wanted for treason, for longer than Vance or Kadee had been alive.

"We need to stop Misha," I said, though the words threatened to choke me. I had done so much to save my sister, but in the end it had been for nothing. No, worse than nothing. Her madness endangered us all now.

"Do we?" Aika asked thoughtfully. "I don't approve of her methods, but she is the one who is supposed to—"

"I'm sick of *prophecy*," Kadee snapped. She addressed the words not to Aika, but to me, as the Obsidian guild's prophet. "I'm sorry, but I am. I'm sick of us following what some vision says. We sold the avian princess to Midnight to buy Misha. Vance and I just helped the Shantel sell the *sakkri* to Midnight—"

"You didn't have a choice," Aika interrupted. "Midnight would have—"

"I don't care what Midnight would have done. I know what *we* did," Kadee spat, "and what we did was give the Shantel's most sacred, revered witch to the vampires. I have nightmares about the feel of her blood on my hands. Now Misha and Aaron are working to sell Hara Cobriana to Midnight. If we continue this way, pretty soon every royal house of the shapeshifters will be owned by the vampires."

I flinched as Kadee listed the atrocities in which we had participated, all in less than a year. Slave-trading, even when it was wrapped in the most noble of excuses, left a dark mark on the soul.

"If we can't warn Hara directly, can we reason with Aaron?" Vance asked. "Misha may be—"

He broke off, looking at me, as if afraid to speak ill of my family member.

"Misha is . . . gone," I said. "My sister is gone. I knew it even before we bought her freedom, or, I *should* have known it, but I was too blinded by what I wanted to be true. Whatever they did to her in Midnight, it didn't make her a slave, but it made her hollow."

"What hold does she have on Aaron?" Vance asked me.

"Misha has no conscious magic," I answered, "but she is a white viper." *Like me.* Both sides of my parentage had a history of black magic. "Her power isn't active, but it is strong, especially now when it is guided by madness and fury. It will seek to protect her, even if that means manipulating the minds of those around her. I do not know how long she worked on Aaron, but he is certainly under her spell."

I wasn't above magically manipulating an enemy into looking the other way or treating me more generously than I deserved, but where I used my magic as armor to protect myself and my kin, Misha had discovered how to use hers as a sword. Every time I looked at Aaron, I could see where Misha's magic had seeped into his mind, twisting his thoughts and bending his will to hers.

"Then we're back to needing to warn Hara," Kadee said. "I know no one here loves her, but I would rather see her on the throne than Misha and her toy king. How does Misha expect to fight Midnight if she starts off by selling someone into it?"

"Fight fire with fire?" I suggested. "The ends justify the means? I don't know what is in her mind. I don't care to."

Liar, I thought. I knew exactly what was in my sister's mind, because I had seen it. She and Shkei had been slaves in Midnight for months. I knew the faces of those who had abused her and left her a creature of wrath and agony who would strike out against any hand that moved toward her, whether they meant to assault or help her. If I ever started to believe my sister's words—that she was fighting Midnight, fighting injustice, tyranny, and slavery, and that the ends justified the means—I needed only to look at the way she had magically enslaved her own declared mate to remind myself that her true thirst was for vengeance and control, not justice or safety.

"I don't know how we will get Hara to listen to us, but I can get us into the palace without the guards capturing us," Kadee said. "I used to know every passageway in and out of that palace, ways even the guards never knew existed. They can't have discovered and sealed them all."

After she had been taken from her human parents, Kadee had been raised as a ward of the serpiente royal family. She had given up that life when she had chosen to protect Shkei from a royal guard.

She had become a criminal to protect my brother.

I had become a mercenary to save my sister.

Shkei was now dead, and Misha was becoming a tyrant.

Weren't we doing well?

And here I was supposed to be a prophet.

"I agree that we should try to warn Hara," I said, "as long as Kadee knows a way we could feasibly do so without getting caught." I took a deep breath and added, "What we need to ask ourselves is if we are *willing* to get caught, if that is what it takes to deliver the warning." I wasn't eager to risk my life to save the serpiente princess, but I wasn't sure how far the others' frustration and guilt would push them.

Aika scoffed. "Are you forgetting that Hara is the one who sent the guards that killed Farrell? We don't even know if the others are alive or dead now." Her voice wavered just slightly, no doubt as she considered her mate, Torquil. "I trust Misha like I trust a bobcat, and I want nothing to do with Midnight's slave-trading, but I don't owe Hara anything."

The faces around me were hard, but not self-sacrificing. We were a group of survivors, and survivors did not risk their lives for abstract things like principles. Food, rest, warmth, companionship, maybe, but high moral ground and ideals? No, those could fall by the wayside, as they always had.

CHAPTER 2

"CAN YOU DRAW *a map of the passages?"*

Kadee bristled, straightening. "You don't need a map. I'm going with you."

Another day, it would have made me smile to watch the fourteen-year-old serpent square off with Aika. Now all I could think about was how I had failed Misha and Shkei. I had been away, and they had been captured. I could only pray that the others could successfully plan to rescue my only living blood kin.

"You're not a fighter," Torquil argued with Kadee, his calm tone cutting through the tense air. "Let someone else—"

"I'm going," Kadee said flatly. "Shkei saved my life. He's my best friend. And I'm the only one who won't get caught getting into the dungeons to save him. Aika, you're good, but even you'll lose if you face an entire dungeon full of palace guards. We don't

need a fighter to go after Misha and Shkei. We need someone who won't have to fight."

"What do you think, Malachi?" Farrell asked, cutting into the argument. "Stealth or strength?"

I tried to make my inconsistent magic serve me. If Kadee went into the palace dungeons, would she be able to rescue Misha and Shkei? Or would she be caught, and lost, as they had been? Would Aika do any better? Or were all our plans doomed to fail?

My power just coiled inside me, useless.

I didn't know, so Kadee won the argument. In the end, it didn't matter. She didn't get caught, but she returned pale and beaten anyway.

"Julian sold them," she whispered, spitting the serpiente king's name with venom I had never before heard from her lips. "I was too late to do anything. They've already been taken to Midnight."

Last summer, we had discussed ways to get into the palace to rescue my brother and sister, without knowing it was already too late. Now we needed to get inside again in order to warn Hara. My magic might be strong enough to let me sneak in, but it would never convince the princess to trust me. Once again, Kadee was the only one with a chance of success.

"What do you recommend?" I asked.

The girl's hazel eyes widened in surprise. "I thought . . ." She trailed off, looking around, as if waiting for others to speak up against one of our youngest members endangering herself. No one did, so she drew a deep breath. "We should—"

I placed a hand on her arm to silence her as I sensed someone approaching through the trees. I tensed, reaching out magically to strengthen the illusion that should keep us hidden.

"Guards?" Aika whispered.

"Vampire," I answered as I recognized the distinct power.

When I saw Aika reach for a weapon, I shook my head. Serpiente guards were dangerous to us, but Midnight's people shouldn't be, unless we did something dumb like threaten them.

I knew the man who stepped into view from my many past visits to Midnight, but that wasn't why seeing him now made my blood run cold. This was the mercenary who had taken Misha and Shkei "off Julian's hands" like troublesome stray cats and brought them to Midnight. Rainwater had made his black hair slick and plastered his clothes to his shadow-dark skin, but he seemed unconcerned by that as he looked around, fingers moving over a talisman in his hand that pulsed with unfamiliar magic.

That hint of power warned me an instant before he turned directly toward us, his gaze shattering my protective illusions.

"Morning, Vance," Nathaniel said, pocketing the

charm that had broken my spell. Clearly, the mercenary had been looking for us, and had even purchased expensive magic in order to find us, but I couldn't imagine why. "Kadee, Malachi, Aika, pleasure to see you all." To my knowledge, Aika and Nathaniel had never met, but he was a mercenary; it was his job to know who people were.

"There's no business for you here," I managed to spit out. The words were not as satisfying as a blow would have been, but they were less likely to get me picked up and thrown into Midnight as well.

"Come talk with me, white viper," Nathaniel said. "Just the two of us."

Aika's sharp laugh answered for me. Aika, Vance, and Kadee weren't the type to be left behind if they didn't want to be. They also weren't quick to trust vampires or mercenaries.

"I know all about Misha's plan," Nathaniel said. "Including the deal she made with Gabriel. Do you?"

The words sent chills through me. Gabriel was one of Midnight's trainers—specifically, the one who had owned Misha for several weeks last fall. I knew she had spent some time in his company more recently. Supposedly, Misha had gone to Midnight to look for Vance and Kadee, who were there trying to help the Shantel untangle a debt left by a failed attack one of their witches made on Midnight. In the end, Kadee and Vance had no choice but to facilitate the sale of the Shantel's holy sakkri—a spirit-witch whose power let her commune with the land and whose gift of prophecy enabled her to advise the royal house—to Midnight. Now I feared Misha may have done a little slave trading while she was there as well.

"I'll speak with you," I agreed as I considered the possible implications of that meeting. "Vance, Kadee, Aika . . ." I trailed off, not sure they would let me send them away.

"See what he wants," Aika conceded. "We'll stay here and work on a plan to get to Hara."

Kadee nodded agreement. Vance asked, "Do you need backup?"

"I should be all right," I answered. "I'll meet you back here."

Nathaniel and I walked farther into the woods with the cool rain sliding down our skins.

"You're the one Misha hired to pick up Hara," I guessed once the others were out of earshot. I wanted to be wrong. How could Misha make a deal with the man who had once sold *her*, as if her value could be calculated in the same way as a bolt of wool?

Nathaniel nodded. "And she has arranged for Gabriel to purchase her."

"Which means the deal has already been made," I said with a sigh, "and our standing in the way of it would be impeding trade."

Midnight's high crimes may have been merely economic, but like anywhere else, they carried stiff penalties.

Impeding the trade of a royal-blood serpent would carry the cost of replacing her value . . . and none of us was royal in blood. I had already been deemed worthless to Midnight, and Aika was too scarred to be acceptable by Jeshickah's standards. Vance . . . I was not sure what they would do to Vance. When they had given up on keeping him as a slave, they had made it very clear that they thought he had the makings of a trainer. Kadee would be considered most valuable, but she was still far from royal. If we interfered with Hara's sale, Midnight could claim all of us.

"Good, I have your attention," Nathaniel said. "Now listen very carefully, because I am only going to say this once:

"It is too late for you to save Hara. That deal is made, and I cannot renege on my word without causing too much suspicion. But if you are interested, I have another deal I want to bring you in on." Nathaniel put up his hand when I started to object. "No, don't give me the speech. You'll like this one better than the last."

"Every deal is 'better than the last,'" I bit out. "You may not be a trainer, but you're still one of their ilk."

"What if I told you that letting Hara go is the first step on the path to seeing Midnight fall?" Nathaniel asked, so softly I was sure I misheard him.

"I would tell you you're mad," I choked out. "How is that even . . ." I looked around instinctively, afraid of being overheard discussing treason against both the serpiente *and* Midnight.

"My employer is paying me a great deal of money to engage in a great deal of risk to bring the end to an era." Nathaniel spoke slowly, as if that would make his impossible words more comprehensible. "If I understand correctly, that has been your goal for quite some time. Incidentally," he added, "did your vision ever say that Misha being on the throne would be the *cause* of Midnight's fall?"

"Prophecies are never that clear," I answered vaguely.

Was he really saying what I thought he was?

Was the mercenary who worked as one of Midnight's strong hands telling me that he had been hired to destroy the empire?

"Will you work with me?" Nathaniel asked.

Did I dare respond?

"I should talk to the others," I hedged, trying to fish for more information, any hint of whether he was sincere, or if all this was some kind of elaborate trap. When we exchanged Alasdair for Misha last winter, we learned that the vampires were sometimes willing to go to extreme lengths to get their way without technically breaking their own laws.

"Yes or no, Malachi Obsidian? On your name and your falcon blood, yes or no?"

No! How could you think I would be naive and suicidal enough to agree to such a thing?

Yes! How could you think I would be selfish and gutless enough to refuse?

I pictured Misha, covered in bruises and shame, staring at me vacantly when she returned to us after months of abuse by the vampires. I thought about Shkei, who had never come home at all, but had died last winter in a trainer's cell. Midnight had destroyed them both.

I remembered all the blood I had helped wash from marble. I remembered my hollow-hearted mother, who had been broken as a slave years before my birth; I had never known who she was when she was free, only what the vampires had turned her into.

I imagined Hara Kiesha Cobriana, who—too soon, it seemed—would be in that same position. Even Aaron was a victim of this juggernaut, chained to Misha for as long as she found him useful.

On your name and your falcon blood.

Nathaniel knew there were not many ways to hold me to my word, but the falcon portion of my heritage could magically enforce vows. I would get myself into trouble if I swore to this path and then decided to turn aside.

If he was trying to entrap me, then telling the mercenary *yes* would get me enslaved—along with my allies—and I would probably not survive. If he was sincere, then I was a threat to him, in which case telling him *no* would certainly result in my death, as well as the deaths of my allies who had seen him with me.

"My magic will bind me to my word, but it will not necessarily bind my people."

"Kadee, Vance, and Aika might tell me to go to hell, but they wouldn't speak up against me," Nathaniel said with a sigh. "You're the only one in that group who might see the profit in turning around and selling me to Jeshickah."

"If I'm such a *threat*," I spat, offended that he would even for a moment think I might favor profit over Midnight's fall, "then why speak to me at all?"

"Because you're a seer," the mercenary said, "and you're a man of magic. I need prophecy and power on my side if I am to succeed, and if I cannot have Farrell Obsidian of the Obsidian guild, or Misha the would-be queen, I want the white viper who first prophesized that Midnight would fall in this generation."

"Why not Misha?"

"Because I trust her even less than I trust you," Nathaniel shot back. "The trainers didn't put enough time into her to break her completely, but I have no faith that she'll be reasonable or predictable with regards to Midnight. More importantly, I need her to rule. The prophecy said she will be queen when Midnight falls, so I need her on the throne."

"Which means you won't let anyone rescue Hara."

He shook his head.

I stared at him, so resolute, and the words I knew I needed to say burrowed into my stomach, through its lining, and into my guts to twine there tightly.

"I'm still waiting on your answer, Malachi," he said.

25

The choices were certain death or likely death, with the possibility that Midnight could be destroyed. But he didn't know . . . no one knew . . .

I opened my mouth to swear, but the words were stifled by a terrible truth, which I needed to utter first.

"It's a lie."

I knew I had whispered, but the words seemed so loud, like they were echoing all around us, heard by everyone who had fought, died, or killed based on my prophecy.

"It's all a lie," I said again. The air felt thick now, choking, and the rain seemed to find its way into my nostrils to slide coldly down my throat into my constricted lungs. "I was seven, and I knew Jeshickah was planning to put me down. Farrell was just going to walk away, so I said what he wanted to hear. I said it because I knew it would make him take us with him. I didn't even know what it *meant*, I just said it and later I convinced myself—"

Nathaniel stepped forward and clapped a hand over my mouth.

"I don't believe in prophecy," he said softly, "but everyone around you *does*. I'm having enough trouble convincing my allies we have a chance after what happened to the Shantel, but the famous Obsidian prophecy, combined with Misha's unexpected rise to the throne, is enough to turn skeptics into believers. So do us all a favor, and *keep lying*. And give me your word that you're on our side."

I nodded, and he took his hand away.

"You have my word," I said. "On my blood as a falcon." *My liar's blood.* "It will be hard to convince Kadee, Vance, and Aika to work with you, though. They're not the most trusting people to begin with, and they won't like that we can't save Hara."

"You've made worse sacrifices," Nathaniel said.

I flinched. "I have."

"Talk with your people," the mercenary said. "Convince them. Then meet with Misha. Convince *her* you've changed your mind. I need you to make sure her plan to take the throne succeeds. Once that is accomplished, I will speak to you about the next steps."

Uneasy allies, we shook hands in the pouring rain. With the handshake, I condemned a royal serpent to slavery, on nothing but the *hope* that someday the hell we were about to send her to would see its end.

CHAPTER 3

I DROPPED TOWARD *the black iron gates of Midnight without the same confidence I had felt when leaving the Obsidian camp. The shapeshifter guards ignored me; I had come and gone so many times in the past decade that they recognized me and considered my arrival unimportant.*

Their disregard made my bones ache with shame, because it meant they considered me essentially one of them: one of Midnight's people, and a traitor to my own kind.

They were right.

Every time I returned to the Obsidian camp, I promised myself that was it. I threw myself fully and sincerely into life as a child of Obsidian. Months would pass, or even a year, but eventually contentment and the flush of freedom faded into restlessness, anxiety, and a feeling I could only describe as unraveling. Each time, I resisted as long as I could, but eventually a moment would come when no one was watching and judging me, and I would return to the stone halls of my birth like a carrier pigeon.

My weakness had cost my sister and brother their freedom. At the same time, my access to Midnight meant I was the only person who might be able to get them back.

After I waved down one of the guards to make my request, I waited in the library for hours before one of the trainers deigned to meet with me. The five trainers—Mistress Jeshickah, Gabriel, Jaguar, Taro, and Varick—ruled Midnight day to day and, more importantly, were the ones who controlled the slave trade. If Julian had sold my siblings, one of the trainers now owned them. There had to be a way to make a deal for their freedom.

I was startled when Mistress Jeshickah swept into the room with a look of contemplation on her face. I could have stood and made my request of any of the other trainers, but when I had been a child, this woman's approval was quite literally the only thing I lived for.

I fought the instinct to kneel in her presence. I had done it so many times before, but a child of Obsidian kneels to no one, and I had sworn to myself when I left our camp that I would never again betray that creed.

"The guards say you have requested a meeting with one of us. I have to wonder what could possibly have made my Malachi so bold," Jeshickah mused.

My throat had gone dry. It took me two tries to speak. "Julian Cobriana sold you two white vipers recently," I finally managed to say. "I would like to discuss how much it would cost to buy their freedom."

"Of course you would." Her lips curled in a humorless smile. "White vipers, though not to my taste, have a certain value due to their rare and thus exotic nature. Your guild, on the other hand, has no wealth to speak of. I don't see that you have anything with which to bargain."

"You can have me," I said desperately.

She lifted one black brow. "I didn't want you twenty-two years ago. What makes you think I want you now?"

I lifted my face to the rain, remembering the day Shkei had been born, in the midst of a violent summer thunderstorm. His name came from the old language phrase *sha'Kain*, which meant "to dance with lightning." He had been free and wild.

My little brother didn't believe in vengeance, but I did. If Nathaniel could give me a chance, I would pull Midnight's stones down with my bare hands. First though, I needed to convince Vance, Aika, and Kadee to trust a vampire and sacrifice a cobra.

I wasn't sure which would be harder.

"The answer is no," Vance said flatly, the instant I stepped into the birch grove.

This will go well, I thought.

"I said the same thing at first, but—"

"No," Vance interrupted. "Kadee has an idea how we can—"

"No," I said, my turn to cut him off. "This is—"

"The deal of a lifetime," Vance quipped. "Too good to resist, or too simple to refuse, or—"

"Shut *up!*" I snapped, losing my patience with the paranoid—though justly so—quetzal. "Misha and Aaron have already made a deal regarding Hara's sale. If we interfere, Midnight will take us all."

Vance let out a barking *caw*. "*Damn* Midnight," he said. "Can't we ever just do what's *right?*"

"And end up in a cell the next day?" Aika cut in. "Though at least you'd die there. Kadee and I would live, which would be worse."

"There has to be some way we can work around the rules to get a warning to Hara," Kadee insisted.

"This is bigger than Hara," I said.

"Tell us what the vampire had to say," Aika said.

"And then we'll decide what to do," Kadee added. Obviously, she didn't intend to let me convince her.

"Nathaniel has been hired," I began, "to destroy Midnight. He asked for my cooperation, and I have agreed to side with him."

My words fell into the day, and were met at first by silence. Barely a breath. We had all seen how dangerous it was to stand up to Midnight. The Shantel had come the closest to success lately, when they had successfully infected all the trainers with what should have been a deadly plague. Unfortunately, the vampires had recovered, and Midnight's wrath had cost them dearly. Could Nathaniel do better?

"That's mighty vague," Aika said at last. "What does he want *us* to do?"

"I don't know all the details," I admitted, "but his first task for us is to make sure Misha takes the throne. He knows about the prophecy."

There it was again, that damn noose of words I had spun so many years ago and could not seem to free myself from now. But the truth I had been willing to give the vampire was more than I could share with the last scraps of my family. I could not bear to know what they would think.

"The Shantel say prophecy doesn't work like that," Kadee said. "A prophecy—a true prophecy, anyway—will come true one way or another."

Aika came to my defense. "Maybe Shantel prophecy works that way, but falcon visions don't. They show a possible future, not a certain one. Right, Malachi?"

I wondered when she had looked into the mechanics of falcon magic. Had she doubted, at some point? Had Farrell, or another member of our group, reassured her with that explanation?

"It's true," I said. "I'm not entirely convinced that everything the sakkri says is inevitable, either, but I know that my visions are not." For how many years had I danced with the truth this way? "What I've seen is a possibility, though. I think the best chance we have to ensure it as a probability is to work with Nathaniel."

"What about Misha?" Vance asked. "Your prophecy named her as the one who would destroy Midnight, didn't it?"

Again, Aika answered, her voice not impaired by the qualms of conscience that made it so hard for me to speak on this subject. "It said she would rule at the time when Midnight fell, not that she personally would cause the fall."

"Then it doesn't matter if she rules," Kadee insisted, "or if we save Hara." Kadee had been raised in part by the royal house. Though she had left there cursing them, Hara and Aaron had been like siblings to her once. "If we cannot go to Hara to warn her, what if we go to Aaron? Malachi, can your magic break him away from Misha's?"

"Maybe . . . But if Aaron is the one who stops the sale, he's the one Midnight will take. I won't sacrifice Farrell's son to save Julian's daughter," I said bluntly. Not even to bring down Midnight, not when the boy Misha had ensorcelled was no more responsible for his actions than a slave in the vampires' empire.

"I'm with Malachi," Aika said. "Prophecy or no prophecy, I won't endanger Aaron to protect the cobra who sent soldiers to murder us. I may not approve of slave-trading, but if I had Hara in my sights, I could kill her without losing any sleep. We still don't even know how many we lost in her attack. If Torquil—" She set her jaw. "We don't know how much Hara has to answer to, yet."

Torquil had once been a swiftly rising star among the serpiente. I didn't know the details of his falling-out with the dancers' guild, except that it had been messy enough to send him rushing into the arms of the Obsidian guild. He and Aika had been inseparable since.

It was hard for me to imagine that Torquil had intentionally gone the opposite way as his mate, but everything had been so confusing during that fight. Had he run with Misha, assuming Aika would go the same way, or had he been cut down in the woods by the soldiers chasing us?

When no one responded to argue or agree, Aika added, "Besides, letting Misha sell a cobra seems a small price to pay if it gives us a chance to destroy Midnight."

"It's not a small price," Vance sighed. "But I don't see any other choice."

Kadee reached out and put a hand on top of Vance's. "I hate this," she said. She drew a shaky breath and let it out slowly. "Fine. It's one more sin on our souls—don't think it's not—but I'll risk explaining myself to God someday if it means I can help set Midnight aflame."

Someday, my sister, you will be queen. When you and your king rule, you will bow to no one. And this place, this Midnight, will burn to ash.

I knew those words had been lies when I spoke them, but that lie had been powerful enough to bring a white viper nearly to the throne—something that had seemed impossible only a few days earlier. Now I could see faith in Kadee's eyes. She believed, and so she was willing to stand with Nathaniel and fight.

Twenty-two years ago, I had lied to save my life.

Now I was willing to die if I could make those words the truth.

CHAPTER 4

I WALKED LISTLESSLY *around the outskirts of our camp, re-*
inforcing the magic that hid us from hostile outsiders . . . the magic
I had allowed to weaken while I was in Midnight, enabling
Julian Cobriana's soldiers to find the people I loved most.

I slid down to sit with my back to the strong trunk of an as-
pen tree, and sucked in a heavy breath. One of its golden leaves
quivered to the ground, another reminder that fall was here. Soon
I would face my first winter alone.

Not alone, *I tried to tell myself.* You have Farrell, and the
others.

It isn't the same.

Though I was most familiar with the five trainers, I recog-
nized the vampire who appeared before me immediately. Acise
was one of Jeshickah's two sisters. I had never actually seen
Katama, though I had been told she was Jeshickah's birth-twin;

she preferred to deal with distant economic affairs instead of involving herself with the local slave trade. Acise likewise spent little time at Midnight, but when she did, she worked as a mercenary.

Without preamble, Acise announced, "I have a business proposal to discuss with your guild."

"I don't think our guild has any interest in any business you might propose," I said in a shaking voice as I stood.

"What if I could offer you one of your white vipers back?"

My world reeled. In that moment, I would have agreed to just about anything.

"What's the price?" I asked.

"Gabriel wants a hawk. Specifically, Alasdair Shardae, the avian queen's younger daughter. She's freeblood, so we can't just pick her up, but if she happened to be offered to us by another shapeshifter . . . well, Gabriel would be certain to offer fair trade, a shifter for a shifter."

I whispered, "There are two of them."

Acise shrugged. "He's only interested in one hawk," she said flatly. "Choose. And act fast. The longer the trainer is bored, the less you will be able to salvage."

From the darkness of the caves, I reached out magically for Misha. I had done so a thousand times when she had been in Midnight. I knew that the first trainer who had owned her and Shkei, Taro, had mostly neglected them—he had been busy tending to Vance, though I hadn't known that at the time. The true abuse hadn't begun until Gabriel had purchased them to use as currency for a deal my guild could not refuse.

Once, I could have reached my sister from across the globe just by closing my eyes. These days it was a struggle to determine where her group was camped. My magical connection to her now was like a rope that had spent too long on a ship at sea. It was tattered and torn, and would leave splinters in the hands of anyone who tried to climb it.

The sea analogy was not mine, or hers. It came from Gabriel, who had left so much of his will overlapping Misha's that little bits of his mind sometimes came to me when I reached for her.

We traveled most of the night, and reached Misha's camp while the dawn birds were still shouting as if to wake the distant sun.

The first person we saw wasn't the would-be queen, but a slender man whose soft features and unassuming grace made him appear younger than he was: Torquil. He took one look at Aika and a grin lit up his face. They flung themselves into each other's arms, the display of affection certainly more sincere than anything I was intending to say to Misha.

Vance and Kadee hung back, seeking each other's hands as they followed me. While Aika and her mate reunited, I found my sister, who watched me approach with a cool gaze and a dagger in her hand.

"How do you come, Malachi?" she asked me.

"In peace," I answered. I drew a deep breath, setting the stage mentally in a way that was more than self-preparation. I visualized the words around me, giving them power. Before now, I had only used my magic on Misha to calm her trembling when night terrors had savaged her sleep and woken her screaming and pale, but I knew she could not defend against it despite her own white-viper blood.

"You and I started this together." I thought of leaving that cell as a child, with my hand not in my mother's but in Farrell's. "I do not like the plan you made with Aaron, but if you force me to choose you or one of the damn royals, I'll choose you. You're my sister, and you're Obsidian."

Except that you want to be queen, even though the Obsidian guild has no king or queen. I tried to keep my doubts far away from the rope of magic I was weaving around Misha. Instead, I thought things like, *Trust me. I am your brother. I am your blood. Remember, I sold a woman of royal blood in order to rescue you. Forget that I have hated myself for it ever since.*

Kadee, Vance, Aika, and Torquil all watched and waited as Misha evaluated my words. The rest of our guild numbered less than a half dozen, and I was sure they would follow Misha when she decided, as they had this far.

If Misha rejected us, we would need to run again. I did not want to know if she would or could stir the others to deadly violence against us. The fear that she might try was sufficient.

At last she stood, and with what might have become a smile in better times she reached out her empty hand to clasp mine. She pulled me close, and I hugged her, daydreaming for a moment that she was still the powerful, proud woman I had been so certain she would be forever.

For you, I thought.

I would betray this woman if I had to, but I would do it for the woman she had been, the woman that Midnight had shattered and put together in a new and vicious form.

"You are the one who brought us this far, Malachi," she whispered to me. "You and Farrell. I thought that losing both of you so quickly might kill me, but you of all people know we need to do this. It was your vision first, after all.

"Hara deserves what she will get," she added, stepping back from the embrace but never dropping her gaze from mine. "She preaches peace while selling her unwanted dissenters into slavery. She cannot remain, not if we want the serpiente as a people to remember who they are, what they are. We are supposed to be a people who worship freedom as our highest divinity.

"Isn't that right, Vance?" she asked, looking up at the quetzal. "You were not born a serpent, but you were born a breed that *cannot* physically live in a cage. You know what it is like to be willing to batter yourself against the bars until you bleed and break, rather than die a prisoner. Serpents have lost that.

"And you, Kadee. You have told me that the people of your birth, the humans, fought a war so they could be the masters of their own fate. They risked their lives. Many of them lost their lives. You told me about your mother, who walked among the sick and wounded as a nurse, and your father—your *true* father, not the serpent who abandoned your mother and you—who fought in the war and later taught you the words of their Declaration of Independence so you would always know what your parents believed.

"Aika, you lost your first family to terrible violence. You and Torquil are so courageous to be willing to try again, and I know my actions must seem reckless to you when safety is so crucial, but do you really want your children to be born into a world where their freedom is seen as a *commodity*? Or would you rather they live knowing their parents fought to make this world better for them?

"We cannot let ourselves be slaves," she said firmly. "If we do, then we are not serpiente. We certainly are not children of Obsidian. If we do not stand up against Midnight, then we are no better than the bloodtraitors that the other shapeshifter nations call us."

Her words were lovely and logical, spoken with passion and intensity, and I wished with all my heart that I could accept them. I wished I could only see her pale green eyes, and not the coil of pain in her soul that was looking for a place to strike. I wished I could rejoice in her bond to her recently declared mate, without seeing the magic she had wrapped like a noose around his throat. Most of all, I wished I could trust her passionate words about Midnight versus the Obsidian guild. But how could I believe anything from a woman who had committed us all to slave-trading without our consent?

To be a child of Obsidian didn't just mean refusing to bow to a king. It meant acknowledging that you had no right to rule anyone else either. Misha had violated the second half of that philosophy.

I swallowed twice and let Misha's words wash over me, using my own power to keep her magic from snagging in my flesh, and doing my best to shield the others. Only when I was sure I could speak with no judgment or anger did I ask, "What is the plan now?"

"The plan . . ." Misha paused, her eyes going distant as she debated whether to trust me. "I purchased a drug from the Azteka that will take down even a cobra. One of Hara's guards will give it to her, and then bring her to us once she is unconscious. I have arranged to meet Nathaniel at a spot in the woods—" She broke off and shook her head. "I'm sorry. It's habit to keep names and details to myself these days. You know the place—where the old hitching posts are. We'll meet Nathaniel there in six days, at sundown. We've arranged for another conspirator to go to the palace with a grievance, so we can be sure that Hara will be where we need her."

I knew her instincts told her not to trust me, but my

power mingled with what she wanted to believe, so she gave me as much information as she could to assuage her own anxiety and prove to herself that I was on her side. For now, she was right.

Torquil and Aika worked together to cook the evening's meal, and we all took stock of what—and who—we had left. The mood was subdued as we all refused to think or talk about what the future held.

Farrell's absence was the most palpable, but he wasn't the only one we had lost. Four other members of our guild were missing; I hoped some of them had just decided to disappear rather than stand up against Misha's plans, but I feared they were more likely to be dead. That left ten of us, not including Aaron, who was currently at the palace.

I was walking the camp's perimeter when Torquil caught up to me, distressed.

"What's wrong?" I asked.

"Some of us were talking with Misha about having a mourning ceremony for Farrell." He spoke in a hushed, careful tone. That, combined with the worried glance he cast over his shoulder in the direction of the campsite, made it clear that the debate had been contentious.

"Misha isn't ready to mourn," I said. She and I had not spoken on the subject, but I knew I was right. Mourning meant remembering someone as they had been. It meant acknowledging the empty space left by their absence. Misha had lost too much of herself. If she ever tried to stare into that void in order to honor her grief she would suffocate. "I don't think I'm ready either," I added.

I had spent the last year as if in a spider's web. I had watched my sister's mind rot. I had felt my brother die. I had seen Farrell fall, on the basis of my selfish words, and now I was witnessing the death of the Obsidian guild. There was too much to mourn, and so little of it could be acknowledged aloud.

"You were closest to him," Torquil said. "If you need to wait, then we will wait. But when the time comes, tell me we will come out here, to the woods? We won't go somewhere like the mourning hall in the palace."

"We'll honor him in the open air, just as he always lived," I assured him. "Has Misha said otherwise?"

"She thinks we should have the ceremony after the coronation, in the palace, because it was Farrell's dream to see us all there," Torquil whispered.

I shook my head, just a fraction, and tried to repress a shudder.

"Misha forgets," I said, "that a child of Obsidian kneels to no king, or queen, even one of our own blood. If Farrell had lived to see Misha take the throne, he would have watched her coronation with pride, and then walked back into the woods. He would not have bowed before her."

Torquil nodded, but there was a new wariness in the response. His tone was guarded as he asked, "And do you expect us all to do the same?"

I blinked at him, aware of the sudden tension between us, but not sure I understood it.

"I'll miss the stars," Torquil said carefully, "but I joined the Obsidian guild because I crossed Julian and the dancers' guild, and refused to beg their forgiveness so they would let me stay. Once Misha's in charge, I'm not going to object to having four walls around me when the winter winds blow or a roof over my head when it pours. If fate finally grants Aika and me children, I don't want them to grow up resigned to cold and hunger and fear."

It was clearly important to him that I understand his motivation; he didn't realize I never could.

"Four walls and a roof," to me, might as well be a cell. I had no misty, sentimental memories of walls or a roof over my head.

But the others had lived different lives. Kadee had been raised in a home with loving parents. Vance had been raised with beautiful walls made of colored glass. Aika had kept a home once, and Torquil had lived in the dancers' nest, where the food and wine flowed like ambrosia and the central fire always burned.

Did they all dream that, once this dirty business was done, we would return to those fantasy lives?

"I guess I hadn't thought that far ahead," I said honestly. It had never occurred to me that the others might see the palace as an end in itself, instead of just the means to one. I fell back on the old creed, though in this context it felt like paste in my mouth. "But either way, why would I be contemplating *your* future? You're a child of Obsidian. If you wish to live with your family inside palace walls, that is your choice to make, not mine."

I supposed a child of Obsidian even had the right to follow a king and queen if he chose; our way was one of freedom, not limitations. That wasn't a choice I could ever comprehend, because there wasn't a monarch alive I had ever viewed as anything but abusive and selfish, but Torquil would make his own decisions—and I would make mine. He would follow Misha even if she claimed a crown. I had other plans.

In the end, that was all that mattered.

CHAPTER 5

THE CAMP LAY *under a smooth bed of snow and ice and the serpents within it ringed tightly around a feeble fire. Finding dry wood had been difficult after the early-winter storm caught them all off guard.*

Malachi stared into the tiny, flickering flames. Around him, he could vaguely sense the others moving, but his mind was far away. He was in a dark cell, where his brother and sister were waiting with dread for the trainer's attention to turn to them again.

Farrell sat next to him. His once-brilliant aura had faded into a dismal swirl of dashed hopes and sacrifices made for what seemed like no reason. He, too, stared into the fire as he said, "Everyone's ready."

Malachi nodded, and forced himself back into this place and time. Now that all their members had gathered, it was time to

49

vote. They had not needed to cast ballots about whether or not to engage in slave-trading because no one had even considered objecting to the trainer's deal. The hawk he asked for was a stranger to all of them, and a royal; the white viper he offered in return was their kin. No, what they needed to decide was which of their people they would save.

"He's only interested in one hawk," *the mercenary had said, when she offered her deal.* "Choose."

They could bring home their brazen, prophesied queen, Misha, or they could bring home Shkei, their youngest and most innocent member.

Farrell handed two small stones to each of them—one dark, and one light—and then held a sack out so they could drop their stone in.

"White for Misha," Farrell said. "Black for Shkei."

At Farrell's insistence, they concealed their votes from the others. However the vote went, Farrell didn't want the white viper who came home to know who chose freedom and who chose death.

Malachi's hand shook as he dropped his black stone into the dark bag, where it let out a dull and hopeless thunk *as it hit the others. He knew his little brother would not win this vote.*

He didn't need to wait for Farrell to upend the sack and count the stones—twelve white, only two black—and seal Shkei's fate. The Obsidian guild had been told that Misha was the one who could save them all from Midnight. They didn't know that Malachi had lied all those years ago and every day since. They didn't know his lies had now sentenced a sixteen-year-old boy to a life of slavery.

Seven months had passed since we took the trainer's deal and Misha returned to us. Even though the vote had not gone the way I hoped, I was still grateful that the choice of which sibling to save had not been left to me alone—especially when my brother's life had ended barely more than a month later.

As the days passed, and I listened to Misha make declarations about our guild and give orders about where everyone should be and what we should do when we met Nathaniel, I had to choke back a thousand biting remarks. Hara's guards may have physically killed Farrell, but Misha had killed his spirit when she started treating the surviving children of Obsidian as nothing more than tools. I could see Vance clench his jaw and avoid meeting Misha's gaze whenever possible. Kadee took long hunting trips that kept her out of camp for hours at a time.

By the time the fateful day arrived, we were all as tense as bowstrings. Misha and the others split off to join her conspirators, leaving Vance and me to guard the clearing. Time passed slowly but interminably, the only positive aspect being that the rain had finally let up. When I heard movement, I braced myself in anticipation. Some last wild hope in me wanted to believe that when Misha returned, she wouldn't have Hara with her.

But she did. Specifically, Torquil had Hara's unconscious body slung over his shoulder. A man in the uniform of the serpiente royal guard trailed after them, his gaze scanning the woods constantly, and his expression utterly blank. I suspected that, like us, he had been convinced that this needed to be done "for the greater good," supported by a great deal of Misha's magic. I also suspected that he was as or more concerned about the children of Obsidian that he knew were in the woods around him as he was about the possibility that they could have been followed.

Misha looked on as Torquil and the guard bound Hara's wrists behind her back to the ring in the old iron hitching post. At some point many years ago a road had traveled through here. Only the crumbling stone hearth remained from what might have been a wayfarer's hut, a place for travelers to pause for the night and rest out of the elements. Now the iron horse head nestled against Hara's spine. The metal there would keep her from being able to shapeshift once she woke.

I hoped we would be gone by then. I did not want to see righteous fury in her Cobriana-garnet eyes, as if this were not a fate she had inflicted upon others. And I did not want to see fear.

"Our guests are here," I called when I spied the group riding toward us through the trees. Across the clearing, I saw Vance flutter to a higher branch, so his dramatic green plumage would be out of sight when the others arrived.

Nathaniel was no longer alone, which didn't surprise me. Vampires had the ability to transport themselves instantly from place to place, but Nathaniel wouldn't be able to carry a shapeshifter with him, so it was useful to have employees help him transport more difficult "cargo." I recognized the two foxes who had worked with him for years, earning themselves a special level of hatred from most other shapeshifters that even I hadn't achieved, but I did not know the human woman with them.

Her hair was warm brunette and her eyes were nearly the same color, maybe a touch toward hazel, though it was hard to tell because she never looked up. The cast of her facial features was somewhat familiar, but it was the way she kept her gaze on Nathaniel as if he were the only one present that helped me make the connection. I was certain that this woman had been born in Midnight, a slave bred much as I had been. Why had Nathaniel brought her here?

"This the one?" Nathaniel asked Misha, as if there could be any doubt. Hara did most of the tariff negotiations for the serpiente. Nathaniel must have met her before.

Perhaps at the sound of his voice, or from instincts warning her of a predator's presence, Hara stirred. She spoke softly, her words slurred so badly they were incomprehensible, as she struggled against the drug's hold.

The foxes moved closer to Hara, though Misha warned,

"She can't shapeshift completely with metal against her spine, but she can shift enough to be poisonous."

Did Julian give them the same warning about you and Shkei? I wondered, glad that I wasn't on the ground so Misha wouldn't see my expression.

I had wondered before how Misha could stand to work with the same man who had sold her. Now I realized the answer. Vengeance. Hara would see the same faces Misha had, from the mercenary who had picked her up to the trainer who had taken her.

Hara shuddered, and lifted her head. She focused first on Misha, and said, "I saw you with Aaron."

"That you did," Misha replied. "You saw me before then, too. Do you remember?"

Hara frowned. Her pupils were so dilated that she had to be seeing halos around everything. She looked past Misha, trying to figure out what was going on. Her gaze briefly settled on me, dragging an image of the past into my present.

I screamed as the blade sliced into my back.

Out of the corner of my eye, I glimpsed Hara Kiesha Cobriana, the eight-year-old serpiente princess. She shouldn't have been allowed to watch this. Did her father, wielding the blade, not care or had he not noticed the girl lurking in a corner?

I saw her, and saw the way her garnet eyes blazed with hatred. My magic let me glimpse the images in her mind, of the fire that had killed her mother, for which the Obsidian guild had been blamed.

Only when Hara's attention turned elsewhere did I manage to rip myself from the unwanted vision. I could still feel the blade—the serpiente's response to petty crimes, which at that age I had been stupid enough to be caught for—in my skin, and see the young cobra's satisfied expression. For a moment, I couldn't remember why I had wanted to save her.

Then Hara saw Nathaniel, and the drugged flush abruptly disappeared from her face, replaced by ghost-like pallor. She whispered "Dear Anhamirak" under her breath, then lifted her head and looked around with more focus, pausing as she beheld each of us waiting in the woods. "You hypocritical fools," she said. "And *you*," she added to Nathaniel, "have no right. These criminals have been exiled from serpiente society for years. They have no power to sell one of us."

Nathaniel just shrugged. It was a mercenary's job to follow the laws, not explain or justify them. Vance and Kadee had recently made a deal that made it illegal for us to sell anyone in the future, but unfortunately, it had been too late. Misha had already set this up. Even if she hadn't, Aaron was a prince of the serpiente. By Midnight's laws, he had the right to sell any of his people at any time he wanted.

Legally, I reminded myself. *Midnight's laws give us the legal right, but no man or woman ever has the moral right to sell another. Even if she would have gladly done the same to all of us, given a chance.*

Nathaniel spoke to Misha briefly. "Given she would obviously like to kill you all, perhaps you and your people should move on before I untie her." He turned back to the cobra. "Lady Hara, do you ride?"

Hara nodded slowly.

"Lady?" Misha mocked.

"Misha, we're done here."

Misha stiffened as if struck.

She wasn't ready to move on. The violence was still twined within her. She had thought that selling Hara would help, that she would feel some relief, some peace, but there was nothing and now it was almost done.

I dropped down from the tree and crossed to my sister, trying to send out calming thoughts. "Misha, we should get back to camp," I said softly. "I am sure you have plans to meet with your king. There is much still left to do."

"King?" Hara asked, incredulous. She continued as if casually speculating about the weather. "Can you imagine, a child of Obsidian bowing to my illegitimate brother. But I suppose you grew used to having a master, back in—"

With a cry of rage more suited to an animal than a person, Misha launched herself at the cobra. The two foxes tried to grab her, but she fought tooth and claw. I received a swipe of her nails across my face and an elbow in my chest when I intervened, so I backed off, listening to my heart pound.

At this point, Nathaniel could have claimed Misha for interfering with a trade. If he wasn't determined to see her on the throne, to get the support of prophecy behind his wild plans against Midnight, he would have seized her as a bonus.

My whole body chilled when the vampire waded into the fray. Within moments, he had Misha pinned to the ground with a hand on the back of her neck.

"*Lady* Misha," he hissed, speaking very softly and deliberately, "take your people, and go. Now. Or *I* will take your people. Am I clear?"

I looked around at the others. I trusted Vance to stay out of the way if Misha continued to cause problems, and Kadee had refused to be here at all for the trade, but some of the others might be spellbound enough to jump in to protect their future queen.

I drew in a slow breath, consciously making the decision: if Misha forced Nathaniel to respond, I would let the mercenary choose my sister's fate. *Torquil*, I decided. If he tried to get involved, I would grab him and hold him back. Aika would be smart and keep safe as long as he was all right.

I couldn't decide if I was relieved or disappointed when Misha's body stilled, and I felt the wave of red-hot rage inside her start to cool, like lava blackening on the surface despite the molten rock still flowing underneath.

Nathaniel left her in the dirt and returned to Hara.

I offered my hand to Misha, but she shoved herself up on her own and stalked away. She did not look back at me, or at the cobra we had just given away, like a burnt offering on the altar of . . . of what? Freedom from Midnight? We gained nothing from this atrocity but illusions. Nathaniel believed some of his potential allies would be more willing to fight if Misha took the throne, but he was playing them for fools. They didn't know their success was no more assured now than it was yesterday.

Nathaniel's group left in one direction; Misha and her soldiers went the other way. I waited, wanting to put enough space between the others that I didn't need to engage in friendly chatter or pretend I found any of this acceptable.

I thought I was alone, until Vance fluttered to the ground and changed back to human form next to me.

"One of us should go with them," he said, nodding in the direction Nathaniel had taken. "Well, not *with* them, but to Midnight, to make sure Nathaniel is keeping up his side of the deal."

"You volunteering?" I asked drily, only to be surprised when Vance nodded.

"I thought about it all night," he said. "I don't really want to go back to Midnight, but I want to be here with

Misha even less. People are saying we'll move into the serpiente palace if Misha takes the throne, but I don't want
to. Midnight would believe me if I stormed out of here and
told them I was sick of it all."

"What about Kadee?" I asked.

I was thinking in terms of what Kadee would think
when Vance left, but Vance took my words differently. He
scoffed. "Kadee doesn't need me here to take care of her.
She's tougher than both of us put together. She knows
how to protect herself, and more importantly, she knows
how to make up her mind without letting anyone manipulate her. If I stay with Misha and Aaron, I worry I'll end
up believing them."

I debated pressing the point, and asking if he thought
Kadee would trust him after he left for Midnight, but decided not to. Instead, I asked, "You believe you can resist the
trainers better than you can resist one mad white viper?"

"Midnight won't be around much longer," he said. "If
they turn me, you'll put me down."

I put an arm around the quetzal's shoulders, and
pulled him close. The two of us were too much alike.

Vance had spent enough time with serpiente that
physical contact shouldn't have startled him, but coming from me it did. He tensed for a moment, then relaxed
against me.

Far too much alike, I thought when Vance asked, "How
long did you live in Midnight?"

"Farrell bought my freedom when I was seven," I answered.

Vance was too astute for such word games. "When you go there, they do not greet you like a slave sold away when you were seven."

No, they don't. "They don't treat me as well as they treat you either," I reminded him. "Do you ever worry what Kadee would think of you if she really knew you, and all the things that go through your head on a daily basis?"

I had an instant to regret the words, which were stupidly defensive, but Vance caught them and recognized them for exactly what they were—a cornered animal's attempt to draw blood.

"Is that what you wonder, when you sit alone by the fire, staring into the flames?" Vance asked, pulling away so he could look me straight in the eye, assessing. He shook his head. "No, you *know* what the others would think of you, and you know they don't think it of me because I didn't know anything else when I lived in Midnight. You . . . you went back, at some point."

I swallowed hard, because the question put me again inside the memory that Hara had already tried to dredge to the surface.

Thirteen marks. Julian Cobriana, the man I would never call my king no matter what crown he wore, had explained how he had decided upon that number, but I hadn't been listening. I had been struggling not to hear the cries and taste the despair of every criminal who had ever been bound to this table before me. That was my magic, my curse.

When I was finally released, and the palace guards threw me back out into the woods, I heard what they were thinking: "What is the point of letting him live? He'll only be back. It would be merciful to put him down–not to mention safer for the rest of us."

Serpiente worshipped a goddess of freedom, and believed that putting a person in a cage violates the dictates of that divine power, so they didn't lock criminals away. Instead, they had only three responses to crime: reparation in service or coin for pretty slights and sins, execution for high crimes, or thieves' marks, which were cut into a criminal's back as a warning. With imprisonment not an option, there was only one treatment for habitual criminals, so any man or woman who earned thirty marks was put down like a sick piece of livestock that risked infecting the other sheep.

After my one and only direct experience with serpiente "justice," I hadn't been able to stand to go home right away. Instead, I had returned to Midnight.

"I was twelve," I said. "I lived there for three months, then fled back to the Obsidian guild."

"Was that the only time?" Vance asked.

I shook my head.

He didn't press, just waited.

"It doesn't matter anymore," I said.

"Maybe," Vance answered.

61

"What about you?" I asked. "You brought this all up for a reason."

He leaned against one of the trees, pressing his palms against the rough bark. "Dammit," he muttered. "I hate this. I listen to Misha, and she makes so much sense I want to believe her. Then I listen to you, and you make sense, too, but I know that when I go back and I listen to someone like Taro or Mistress Jeshickah, they'll also make sense. So here I am, lying to almost everyone, helping sell a woman I've never even met into slavery, questioning every decision I make . . ."

"Then you're in the exact same boat as all the rest of us," I answered. "I think the only person in our guild who feels confident she's doing the right thing is Misha."

Vance shook his head. He didn't need to say out loud what we all knew about Misha.

"Sometimes I hate you," he said. "I look back, and my life was perfect right up until the moment you walked into it."

I grinned, but it was not a happy expression. "Sometimes I hate you, for the exact same reason. But I think I love you, too."

"Yeah," Vance answered, picking at the bark in front of him idly. "Kadee says it's normal for siblings to want to hit each other occasionally. Is that what we are?"

"We had the same parents," I said. On a desperate rush of breath, I asked, "Can you stand to wait until Misha's coronation before you leave for Midnight? I don't think I can face her every day without you and Kadee with me."

Vance paused to consider and then finally nodded. "Midnight will probably find it more believable if I wait a while and then say I left because I didn't like Misha's leadership, anyway. It won't make much sense to say I left because I disapproved of selling Hara, considering where I'm going."

I didn't know what would happen after Misha took the throne. I didn't know what Kadee would do, or what Nathaniel had planned for all of us. I did know that I would never be able to sleep inside the palace walls, no matter what Misha expected after her coronation. If she tried to force me, I would slip away like Farrell had so many years ago, accept the consequences of that decision, and try my best to live by Obsidian's ideals.

CHAPTER 6

WE HAD TO *stalk the hawk for weeks, learning her habits, before we had a chance to make a grab. Once we did, the abduction was flawless. We escaped pursuit, leaving no trace of what had happened to the younger avian princess. I was so focused on doing what we needed to do to save my sibling that it wasn't until I actually* looked *at her, the golden-haired young woman trembling with fear and rage, that something in me said,* This isn't right.

But by then the deal was made. Acise was there to pick up Alasdair, and she had Misha with her. If she hadn't, maybe I would have been able to speak up to say, "We can't do this," but Misha could hear me, and I could see her, see the bruises on her skin and the blindfold across her eyes and the bonds on her hands, and even though I could sense the aura of madness I could not stand to step forward and say, "No, it isn't worth it."

So we made the deal.

I untied Misha's hands and uncovered her eyes while Acise rode away with the unconscious hawk cradled in her arms like an ill friend she was taking care of.

We all went home. Everyone except Alasdair. It was almost easy. Certainly easier to do than to live with.

As spring's chill started to give way to early summer warmth, greens began to poke up from the damp earth . . . and Misha became increasingly frustrated with her mate.

Watching her argue yet again with Aaron, I couldn't help but think more about the woman we had sold in order to save her. It had seemed so easy to justify my actions then. Now I knew that I had made a devil's deal.

I added Alasdair to the list of victims it was beyond my power to save, and turned my attention to Aaron, wondering if I could do better by him.

"You're stalling," Misha accused him. "I got Hara out of the way for you. It's your turn to be bold now."

Aaron flinched, looking cautiously around the camp as if to confirm that no one outside our guild had heard Misha's words.

"I'm not *stalling*," he replied, his voice calm despite his anxious expression. "Julian and our people don't know what happened to Hara, but they aren't idiots. If I walk in with you right now, they'll know. I've had people I trust planting rumors that Hara made a deal with Midnight and it went bad somehow. It will make her less sympathetic, pave the way for our speaking out against the vampires, and keep us from being the only suspects once Julian hears where Hara is now."

Misha pulled away from her mate and stood. She glared at me as her pacing took her past my spot by the fire, and I looked away, careful not to meet her mossy-green eyes. Like Misha, I was impatient for our plans to move forward, but I also understood Aaron's logic.

If he hadn't been caught in Misha's thrall, I thought Aaron would have made a good king . . . as kings went, anyway. He had Farrell's ability to step back and consider the whole situation, as well as his knack for speaking to people in a way that made them feel valued and respected. If we brought Midnight down, and then separated him from Misha, perhaps he could recover well enough to make both his fathers proud. We just needed to make sure he survived.

Misha paused in her pacing to ask, "What about the trade laws?"

Aaron's frame relaxed, as if he believed this subject was safer than the last.

"Julian is hesitant, but I think I nearly have him convinced. He has started taking an inventory of supplies, and has given me the account books so I can use them to estimate what we will need."

"What are you talking about? What trade laws?" I asked. I would have preferred to be a silent observer, avoiding Misha's attention, but it didn't seem that they were about to divulge the details of this previously unmentioned plan without prompting.

Aaron smiled, as if pleased that I was showing an interest. Misha's eyes narrowed fractionally.

"Kadee gave us the idea, actually, when she negotiated with the Shantel," Aaron explained. "Midnight requires that all commerce take place in public markets, and they tax all transactions that happen there. Our plan is to avoid lining their coffers by refusing to trade."

"People can live without luxury goods," I pointed out, "but what about things like fuel and food?"

Aaron nodded. "That's why the royal house is going to collect all essential goods and organize their fair distribution. No coins change hands, so no taxes are owed."

"It meets the letter of the law," Misha said. "We all know Midnight is fond of splitting hairs until the laws suit them. It's time for us to do the same."

The plan was brilliance, or madness, or some of both, but it had a few major flaws.

"You expect people to simply turn over their possessions and trust you to take care of them?"

This time, it was Misha's turn to grin. "There has already been some resistance. Sadly," she said, with no hint of sorrow in her tone, "we expect threats. We may need to train more guards in order to keep our people under control."

The shapeshifter nations were forbidden from keeping an army, but encouraged to have guards to police their own. Misha was hoping for an excuse to train soldiers.

"How are you going to deal with the fact that the serpiente get most of their food from Midnight?" I asked. The serpiente, like all the local shapeshifter nations, relied on Midnight for basic provisions.

"As soon as I take the throne . . . as Aaron's mate," Misha added, as if he were an afterthought, "I plan to declare that the serpiente intend to refuse all future aid from Midnight. The royal house will ration the supplies we have. The Obsidian guild has plenty of experience surviving on limited resources. We'll manage, until we can break our own fields."

"A dozen thieves can live off the land—and their neighbors' bounty—easily enough," I argued. "That isn't going to work for the entire serpiente nation."

I looked to Aaron, wondering if he could offer better solutions to the obvious problems in Misha's plan. The moment I did, I felt Misha's magic lash out, squeezing the serpiente prince and shoving any independent thoughts he might have aside.

"Do you *hear* yourself?" Misha challenged me as she smothered her mate's potential contribution to the discussion. I saw others look toward us, and Misha's magic twined around them, too. "Midnight is not the only nation with *dirt*. The vampires don't even eat, so why, in two centuries, are they the only ones who have learned how to plant fields of corn or squash? Why are they the only ones who benefit when the rivers run thick with salmon? When we first came here, they offered us food in exchange for the luxury goods our artisans could provide. They taught us to create what we could sell instead of what we could *eat,* and that has made us dependent on them, but we are a nation of people with passion, innovation, and intelligence. What stops us from changing our ways?"

"I'm not saying we can't." Why was I bothering to argue? The glint in her eye made it clear she didn't intend to listen to reason. "I'm saying we might need to go slower. It's already June. We have no cleared fields, and few farmers." The serpiente grew flax for textiles, and a limited amount of oats and wheat—which was mostly used for hay for the sheep—but it wasn't nearly sufficient to feed us all.

Misha closed her eyes and drew a deep, slow breath, then nodded. Instead of feeling relief, I tensed, because I sensed her sudden resolve.

"Excellent idea," she said. I wasn't sure what she was referring to, but I already doubted I would like it. "You can go to Midnight, and to the bloodtraitors' village. Inspect their farms. Serpiente who go to Midnight often do so for the same reason we came to Obsidian, because they were in trouble with the royal house. You can let them know that, once we have a new king, they can earn pardon in exchange for their expertise."

Aaron frowned. "I know Malachi's magic helps him avoid undue attention, but someone will notice if he starts sneaking around—"

"Oh, he won't need to sneak," Misha interrupted. When she fixed her gaze on mine, I could see her fury. No matter how logical my points were, she couldn't stand my challenging her. "Malachi goes to Midnight regularly. I'm not sure what work he does there . . ." She paused, letting damning speculation fill the brief silence. "But they let him stay whenever he wants. They *trust* him."

And with those words, she made certain that Aaron never would. I wanted to defend myself, but what could I say? Except for my efforts to save Vance, I hadn't been back to Midnight since Misha and Shkei were taken, but even to me that sounded like a lame defense.

"Thank you for the suggestion, Malachi," Misha added sweetly. "And you're right, as soon as possible would be best. I'll summon you back when I'm ready for a report."

I opened my mouth to argue, but the look on her face and Aaron's warned me not to.

"You may go," Misha said, as if the dismissal hadn't been clear enough yet. "I'll let the others know where you are."

I'm sure you will, I thought. I looked around for Vance and Kadee, but they had pitched their tents too far away to overhear my argument with Misha. When I reached out with my power, I could sense them curled uneasily together, sharing their fears and fragile hopes in hushed voices. Aika met my eyes briefly when I looked toward her, then turned her back after Torquil said something to her. She was far enough away that she would have heard Misha's raised voice, but not her more quiet orders to me.

There was no subtle way I could confer with any of them before I left without making Misha suspicious and getting my only allies in trouble. I didn't have a choice. I changed shape and left the camp, hoping the others would trust me no matter what Misha told them about my disappearance.

I landed in front of Midnight in the dark hours before dawn, and boldly sought Nathaniel's room. We had recently sold a cobra. It would not seem odd for me to speak to the mercenary we had worked with. Like Misha had said, Midnight trusted me.

I was frustrated to learn that Nathaniel was out. He had told me to stay with Misha and make sure she succeeded in taking the throne, and I doubted he would be happy that she had sent me here; I needed to know what he wanted me to do next. I also wanted his opinion on Misha's mad plan, and how it would be helped or hindered by his own scheme. Midnight wouldn't let her get away with it for long. When was Nathaniel planning to strike?

"Out? For how long?" I asked the woman who answered the door. I recognized her as the second-generation slave who had been with Nathaniel when he picked up Hara.

She responded to his question with a shake of her head. "I cannot answer that," she replied.

Because you don't know, or you aren't allowed to tell? I wondered.

"When did he buy you?" I asked.

Nathaniel had long avowed that he had no interest in keeping personal slaves. This seemed an odd time to break his rule, unless her purchase was somehow related to his plan for Midnight's fall.

"Just over three weeks ago, sir," she replied.

That *sir* had always grated on me, even when I was twelve.

"Would you like me to deliver a message to Master Nathaniel?" the slave prompted. A note of unease had entered her tone, warning me that further questions would draw suspicion. For all I knew, Jeshickah had forced him to take this slave on due to some suspicions of her own. I didn't want her reporting anything unusual.

"Tell him Malachi Obsidian was here to see him," I said, "and that I will be in the building if he wishes to speak to me."

"Yes, sir."

I intended to go to the bloodtraitors' village, both to obey Misha's command and to gather information for myself, but I had to wait until after dawn. The vampires may have been up and alert, but the farmers who worked for them couldn't force their crops to be equally nocturnal. For now, I would find somewhere to sleep for a few hours, so I could investigate agriculture once the sun was up.

I started in the east wing, which held cell after cell of silent slaves, some engaged in work, and others sleeping. The cell where I had been born and lived for the first seven years of my life was currently empty. I stepped inside, drawn by the ghosts of my past, and touched the edge of a wool blanket that had been neatly folded and set at the end of the bed.

Someone lived in this room, but there were no knick-knacks, no symbols of anyone's existence.

I turned around, and a memory assaulted me.

The blow knocked me to my feet, blood at my lip and buzzing in my ears. I didn't understand what I had done wrong, and I couldn't seem to give the right answer—

I struggled out of the mind of some nameless slave who had died many years before at the hands of an angry master or mistress. I had not picked up enough to know the particulars of the death. I didn't want to.

See how the blood flows.

I turned away from that memory, too.

They had put my hands in the blood. I had been taught what a blade could do to flesh. What the slender, seemingly soft leather end of a whip could do. Worse, I had learned what *words* could do, words that could slice the psyche deeper than any dagger or blunt instrument could ever reach. Trainers liked to teach, and I hadn't been able to resist learning, even when the lessons were horrible.

Life in the Obsidian guild was *hard*. Winters were cold, and empty bellies were common. A wrong step meant potentially being caught by serpiente guards and marked by the blade, executed, or sold. And what I could never explain to Farrell, what I would never have the nerve to say to anyone, was that making choices, being wholly responsible for myself every moment of the day, was exhausting. I believed in the Obsidian guild's creed, I really did . . . but it was hard to live by.

No matter what I saw in Midnight, it wasn't until the victims were my own flesh and blood that I had found the resolve to leave for good.

CHAPTER 7

IT WAS SO cold. Shkei's stomach was empty, and his muscles were aching. He didn't shiver; serpents could feel cold, but their bodies did nothing to alleviate it. Instead, the chill seeped into his blood and his bones, leaving him without even the energy necessary to rub his hands together.

He craved warmth as much as he craved light. How long had it been since he had seen the sun? Or heard a voice—of any kind, gentle or not? The slaves who delivered his meals did so in silence. Even the trainer hadn't bothered to speak to him, and though Shkei knew that was probably a good thing, he was starting to feel so desperate, he almost wished the vampire would just do something *already*.

He had no way to tell the passage of time. He didn't know how long Misha had been gone, or whether she was alive or dead.

The door opened to admit a woman who at first was simply a blur against a halo of light.

Shkei flinched, because normally when that door opened, pain followed, but this time it slammed shut again quickly, leaving darkness . . . but warmth. His serpent's senses could feel another form in the darkness, one putting out constant heat.

He could feel the vibration of her shivers in the air.

"Hello?" he said softly, desperately.

Was this another trick? Another trap? Another seeming gift that was going to be snatched away at the last moment?

"He-hello?" she stammered in reply. "Who's there?"

Her voice was like music to him. "I'm not going to hurt you," he said, because if she wasn't one of them, *then she had to be as terrified as he was. "What's your name?"*

"Alasdair."

When I heard Gabriel Donovan's voice, it took me a minute to realize it was here and now, not in the memory of my brother's last days. I looked up in time to see the trainer walk by the cell I was in, seemingly deep in conversation with another trainer, Jaguar.

"I have a meeting now about a possible acquisition or two from Ahnmik," Jaguar was saying. "Are you sure you don't want to join me?"

Gabriel shook his head. "I just took in a new project here, in addition to a major investment to expand my shipping company. I won't have time for a falcon any time soon."

New project. I shook my head in disgust at the way Gabriel referred to Hara, so impersonal. I also made a mental note to ask Nathaniel about Jaguar's falcon when I saw him. When falcons sent criminals to Midnight, they normally bound their power tightly to keep the vampires from using it, but there was still a possibility that he or she could be recruited as our ally . . . as long as I wasn't directly involved. Falcons hated mixed-blood individuals like myself.

There was another powerful magic user we might be able to enlist to help us take down Midnight, and if Jaguar was going from here to a meeting she would be unguarded: the Shantel sakkri. Ever since Kadee and Vance had told me their tale, I had wondered if the sakkri had deliberately manipulated events so she would end up here. Why else would the most powerful figure among the Shantel let herself be sold as a slave? This seemed like an excellent opportunity to get my question answered.

I retraced my steps, and returned as quickly as I could to the west wing. The door to Jaguar's room was locked, but that meant nothing to me; a little magic turned the mechanism, and then I stepped inside.

It was only as I reached for the latch to the back cell that I realized how wrong I had been.

The sakkri wasn't in the cell, as I expected, but sitting

cross-legged on the floor of the main room with her head bowed as if in meditation. I had walked right past her at first, because she had barely registered with my power. She was hollow.

It's been less than a month, I thought. How had the trainer done this much damage, so quickly?

"Sakkri?" I asked.

She didn't respond. I reached for her with my magic, and found a void where hers should have been, like the hole left behind when a storm rips a tree up by the roots.

I knelt in front of her, touching her hand to try to get her attention. Her eyes opened and she looked at me placidly.

"Sakkri?" I said again.

"No." I frowned, puzzled. "I was," she said, "but I severed my connection to the land. Three times. In blood, in land, in name."

"I don't understand." Kadee had said something about the sakkri attacking a member of the Shantel royal house, despite being forbidden from violence and bloodshed, in order to force them to sell her to Midnight. Could that have burned her power from her?

"I am where I need to be," she said. "Please . . . don't ask me for anything else." Her voice broke on the last words, revealing emotion for the first time.

She closed her eyes again, and I obeyed her wishes, backing out of the room as a chill settled over me.

In the hall, I just stood and stared at Jaguar's door, trying but unable to make any sense of what I had just seen. One thing I was sure of: it wasn't just an act for the trainer's benefit. The sakkri might not be broken yet by Midnight's standards, but her own power had gutted her.

I shuddered, and my gaze moved to the next door down the hall. I sensed no vampire behind it, but knew that the victims of my sins were surely there: the hawk, and the cobra. Helplessly, I reached for the knob. I didn't think about what Gabriel would do to me if he found me in his rooms, only about how I needed to know what was left of the first woman I had sold, my brother's last companion.

Hara was probably locked away in the back cell. Alasdair, who the trainer now called Ashley, was curled up asleep in bed with her aureate hair pooled on the pillow around her porcelain face. There were no bruises visible on her flesh, but most of her was concealed beneath blankets. Besides, I had seen plenty of blows, plenty of her blood, through Shkei's eyes. I didn't need to see evidence now in order to know the extent of her suffering.

I stepped closer and her eyes fluttered open, golden lashes framing eyes an even deeper copper. She regarded me first with sleepy confusion, and then with fear as she sat up, holding the blankets around herself as she asked, "Can I help you?"

I want to help you, I thought in reply.

"Do you remember me?" I asked.

I didn't want her to, and I hoped she didn't.

She looked at me, and frowned. I felt my magic waver, as something in her reached out, trying to focus. It was more than I had felt from the sakkri. After a moment, Ashley shook her head. "I'm sorry," she said. "Should I?"

We did not get further before a strong hand gripped the back of my neck hard enough to weaken all my muscles. As my knees collapsed, Gabriel flung me down so that my skull struck the marble floor.

Breath knocked from my lungs and my vision swirling, I was barely aware as he asked Ashley, "Are you all right?"

I did not hear her speak.

"Malachi, you should remove yourself from here," Gabriel suggested.

I half crawled and half stumbled out the door without waiting for my vision to clear. I was foolhardy and often stupid, but even I knew that when a trainer was in a good enough mood to offer a second chance, you should take it. Otherwise he would need to make a point out of principle, and freeblood laws were much less protective once someone put himself in a trainer's territory.

In the hall, I tried to make sense of what I had felt. In those few moments before Gabriel had interrupted, I could have sworn I could feel a free mind, not just the resignation of a broken slave.

Was that a fantasy, a self-deception? A lie my own

power fed me to keep me from despair, as if saving this woman would undo all the sins related to her enslavement?

I knew her as a brave, powerful woman, both from my own memories and from the visions I had seen through my brother's eyes after she was sold to Gabriel. That woman was long gone. She had to be; she had belonged to the trainer since last November, over half a year ago. What I was sensing was probably just an echo of my own visions and wishes.

I was still sitting against the wall of the hallway, struggling to catch my breath, when a pair of vampires approached. I did not go to my knees, but neither did I rise, and obligingly Jeshickah and her cohort ignored me.

"Kendra was not happy with the result of your last meeting," the man reported. "She is threatening to move to Silver's side."

Jeshickah's guest had similar coloring as Vance, dark skin with a rusty hue, and thick black hair. The resemblance was sufficient for me to guess at his identity: Theron.

Theron wasn't Azteka, but had been born among the humans who called themselves the *Mexica*, from whom the Azteka had descended. He was a powerful figure in Midnight, one of the few mercenaries who had *not* been changed by Jeshickah and did not owe her any particular allegiance. He often spoke for Kendra's line—that volatile group of immortal artists—and was regarded as someone who was more reasonable than most of his line, but not to be trifled with.

Jeshickah shook her head. "I hurt Kendra's pride, and she is not a woman who tolerates that lightly, but Silver and his little castle will hurt her *art,* and she will not tolerate that at all. His line's attempt to gain power is like an ancient feudal castle trying to control its serfs. It makes no attempt to trade, or communicate, or—" At last she glanced down at me to say, "Malachi, don't clutter the hallways." I pulled my legs closer to myself, sitting cross-legged so she would not need to step over me, and she turned back to her companion. "Kendra and her line are posturing. They think Silver's offer is better because he proposes more freedom and fewer restrictions. Kendra thinks she can use that as a bargaining chip when she deals with me. She learned last time that she was mistaken, that is all. Come, let's sit. Malachi, fetch us a platter."

I considered objecting, but it wasn't worth a broken rib. Besides, this sounded like a conversation worth overhearing. Who was Silver? Was there already someone in play who might be able to compete with Midnight? Was he the one who had hired Nathaniel? And more importantly, would he be any better for the shapeshifters than Midnight was?

I hurried to obey so I could return and continue listening. When it was Jeshickah and a vampiric guest, a "platter" meant a combination of fruit, chocolate, wine, and two slaves from the current feeding pool to serve it. Tasty foods appealed to the vampiric palate, but they did not provide sustenance. That came in just one form, and only ran through living veins.

"*Brina?*" Jeshickah was saying incredulously as I returned with the snacks. "Brina thinks new things are fun, but she will turn on them as soon as she realizes those ancients do not know what royal indigo hue *is*, much less where to acquire it."

Now that I knew a conspiracy against Midnight was actively emerging, it was interesting to note that the leader of the most hated empire in existence still found the concept that people might turn against her utterly absurd. She clearly dismissed the shapeshifters as an insignificant threat on their own despite—or perhaps because of— recent unsuccessful assassination attempts, and had no doubts about the loyalty of her own kind. Surely there had been *some* hints, somewhere. Had Nathaniel been feeding Jeshickah false information to make her more confident? Or was she so arrogant that she ignored any signs of rebellion she saw?

Or was she right?

I took a seat on the floor next to the couch where Jeshickah sat, and continued to listen.

"She—" Jeshickah didn't question my presence, but Theron paused, and said, "I don't believe I'm familiar with this particular member of your staff, Jeshickah."

"Malachi isn't on my payroll," Jeshickah answered. "He's more like a stray cat who wanders in and out when he likes and doesn't know better than to bite the hand that feeds him."

Her guest's face registered amusement. "Do you have many of those?"

"A few. They serve their purpose, and do no harm."

"Except when they bite?"

"*Especially* when they bite," Jeshickah replied, laughing. She reached down to pet my hair, just as she might reach toward the cat she had referred to me as. The contact—the barest *acknowledgment*—still had the ability to thrill me just a bit. A reflex; that's all it was when my heart skipped a beat. A memory, from years when a gentle acknowledgment from this woman meant everything, meant I had a reason to exist.

"He isn't human," Theron observed.

"Half falcon, half serpent," Jeshickah replied. "Unfortunately, the falcon magic didn't take strongly in the product, and the father did not survive long, so I was unable to test other variations." *Did not survive long.* My father had gone mad, as falcons tended to do even in the best of circumstances. He had nearly killed me and my mother both. It was one of my earliest memories. Jeshickah added, "He seems to have thrived better in the wild, so to speak, than he did in captivity. He has something of a leadership role in the Obsidian guild. They sold us a hawk last winter, and about a week ago they gave Nathaniel a cobra, essentially free of charge."

The mercenary looked at me, and said, "Come here." He was either intrigued because of my falcon heritage, or else he was accurately suspicious about my interest in their conversation—or both, of course.

Most people would have been concerned. Vampires could read thoughts.

They could read them even better when blood flowed, a fact that was not lost on me as Theron pulled me close and brushed the long strands of diamond-white hair back from my throat. He was gentler than most as he cradled the back of my head in one hand, guiding me to bare my throat.

CHAPTER 8

"ARE YOU HURT?" *Shkei asked, rising to his feet. "Physically, I mean." Anyone in this place would be hurt in spirit and heart.*

As he moved closer, Shkei realized that she was too warm to be human. She had to be avian, a bird shapeshifter, which meant that someone–probably someone she knew, maybe even trusted or loved–had sold her into this place. Yes, she had been hurt.

"I'm not injured," she answered. Her voice was soft, precise, modulated, as if she had been trained how to speak. All avians were taught to control their emotions, but her lyrical cadence hinted at further education.

He touched her cheek and she jumped, so he drew back, reminding himself that avians didn't touch casually or for comfort.

She followed, reaching for him in the darkness.

"I hate the dark," she confided, the polished tone momentarily

supplanted by something more honest. "I'm sorry. I never asked your name."

"I'm Shkei," he answered.

She leaned against him, so warm compared to the cold cell and loneliness. He tried not to let her hear him sigh. It was pure evil that he felt even momentarily grateful *that another living being had been put into this hell.*

Grateful . . . and at the same time, full of hatred as he imagined the people who had put her here.

My shame as I felt my brother's revulsion at what we had done to Alasdair far outweighed any discomfort I had about giving blood, though among freeblood shapeshifters I was in the minority.

Others often saw giving blood to be a shameful act, but it meant nothing more to me than sweeping a floor or cooking a meal in this place would have. It helped that, unlike most people, I had no reason to fear the mental invasion that often accompanied it. The particular mixture in my blood turned my mind to a swirling, hallucinogenic vortex—Jaguar's description, from years ago—from which no thoughts could be read.

The pain was brief.

The pleasure of having one's blood drawn was sweet, and seemed to last forever. The touch of the mercenary's mind was enough to make it clear he was from the artists' line despite his profession. He did his best to roll my mind, and I went into the haze willingly, letting myself drift in currents of music and light and color without concern.

When it ended, I regained myself quickly. A vampire's hold could not begin to touch the whispers of a falcon's magic, which I needed to navigate and ignore every instant of my life. Quite the opposite, since most vampires who tasted my blood tended to become incautious and impulsive afterward.

Theron fell backward into the soft, welcoming armchair, releasing me too late to keep me from toppling briefly onto his lap before I righted myself and found a seat on the floor instead. His hand followed me, as if seeking more, and I felt his fingers idly toying with my hair.

I leaned toward him with a silent sigh, justifying it as a means of further dulling his suspicions, though I had personal motives as well. Since Farrell had brought me into the Obsidian guild, I had been raised in a culture that valued touch, but when I was a child, skin-to-skin contact had always brought overwhelming visions. By the time I could control my visions, even newcomers to the guild viewed me as something different, a half-falcon prophet instead of a person, untouchable and remote.

Theron said to Jeshickah, "*That's* why you keep him around."

"That, too," she answered with a soft smile.

"I will have to save a deeper drink for another time, though, since we still have work to discuss."

Jeshickah nodded.

"First order," she said. "I want you to deliver a message to Brina. If she leaves us for Silver's empire, I do expect her to leave behind all property that is not explicitly hers, which does include the 'staff' she borrowed from here and the slaves she has been using as models. Also remind her that her greenhouse is on our land, and subject to destruction should she decide that she does not require our alliance any longer."

The mercenary nodded. Though he seemed more physically relaxed than he had been, I did not doubt that his mind was following every command.

I also had no doubt that Brina would back down after hearing Jeshickah's warnings. The greenhouse was an elaborate affair covering more than an acre, made of a combination of clear and stained glass laid out in dramatic panels, with occasional mesh windows to allow the passage of fresh air. It had been built by Midnight as part of their attempt to raise an Azteka bloodwitch—Vance—in such a beautiful cage that he never realized he was a slave. I suppressed a smile as I imagined seeing it demolished.

The conversation continued along those lines for the next few minutes, with Jeshickah leveling ultimatums against several other members of Kendra's line. I didn't know all the names mentioned, but the overall message was clear: *someone* was fighting for leadership of the vampires. Jeshickah took the threat only seriously enough to make sure her people knew what they would be losing if they tried to defect.

After Theron had been dismissed and Jeshickah had left, I stood. Carefully. I hadn't lost much blood, but it still took a moment for my head to clear.

I had so much I wanted to talk to Nathaniel about, and absolutely no way to contact him until he deigned to come find me. In the meantime, it was nearly sunrise, I was hungry and exhausted, and unlike Vance my occasional visits here did not involve luxurious accommodations.

At least food was plentiful. I helped myself to stew and bread in the kitchen, unchallenged by any of the guards or the broken slaves, who moved around me with wary glances but would not speak unless spoken to first.

I wondered if I should offer to bring the meals down to the west wing, come sundown. The vampires' personal slaves and current projects would eat—or not, as the trainers chose. Ashley and Hara would need food. Bringing it to them might give me a chance to see—

Leave that alone, I tried to tell myself. *It's not worth a beating, or worse, just to get a glimpse of them and make yourself feel like scum.*

Even so, my feet brought me to the west wing, where the mercenary who had met with Jeshickah earlier was just reaching his room.

"Theron?" I said. My understanding was that Theron rarely dealt with slaves, and did not like to be addressed by a title.

He nodded. "Jeshickah tells me you're behind Midnight's recent acquisition of ruling powers from the avians, Shantel, and serpiente."

"I wouldn't put it quite that way."

"Jeshickah does have her own, unique outlook on the world," the mercenary remarked as he unlocked the door to his room. "Come in."

I wasn't sure if the words were meant to be an invitation or an order, but I obeyed, curious. Theron was supposedly a powerhouse of information, involved in everything. Did he know about the plot against Midnight already?

"Congratulations on your sister's rise to power," Theron remarked as he removed his boots and unbuttoned the cuffs of his shirt, making himself comfortable. "I hear that Aaron is pushing to have the coronation ceremony as soon as possible."

The words were spoken casually, but they had the potential to be a trap, so I was careful in my response.

"I am glad Misha was able to persuade him," I answered vaguely, wondering if plans had moved ahead since Misha sent me away or if Theron was commenting on the negotiations Aaron had already been making to ensure her safe rise to the throne.

Moving on from that subject, Theron asked, "Can I get you anything to drink?"

I nodded, mostly to be polite, and to conceal my unease and confusion. I could cover why I had walked into this room with the fact that he had *told* me to, so I was not worried that he could learn anything through my behavior thus far.

"Obedient slave" was an easy role to play, if one had a mind to. People talked around and over slaves, or even at them, without much concern. But they did not usually talk *to* them, and the other thing I knew about Theron was that he did not bother with slaves. So what did he want with me?

Did he suspect I was up to something? If so, did he have any idea how big a plot I was involved with? I didn't know any details about Nathaniel's plan, but the fact that there *was* a plan and one of Jeshickah's own line was orchestrating it was the kind of information Theron regularly bought and sold. If I were willing to betray Nathaniel—not to mention every shapeshifter ever dominated by Midnight—I could probably turn a few words into a small fortune. With Theron as middleman, I would probably even survive to enjoy my rewards.

Did he sense that opportunity for profit? If he did, what was he willing to do to get it? Or was I jumping at shadows? I was the brother of the soon-to-be serpiente queen. That could make me a valuable contact, too.

I tried to wait patiently, telling myself it would be better to let Theron lead the conversation, but anxiety got the best of me. I asked, with only a hint of irritation, "Is there a particular reason you asked me to come in?"

He handed me one of the two glasses, and I took a cautious sip. The drink tasted vaguely like spicy mulled cider.

"Should there be?" Theron replied.

This is why I hate mercenaries, I thought. Did he know something or not?

"If you're hoping I can help you connect with Aaron's soon-to-be queen," I said, "I'm afraid I will not be much help. Our relationship is a bit strained at the moment."

"I gathered, despite your evasion earlier. What seems to be the problem?"

This man was too powerful to lie to on a subject that it was very likely he could and would confirm, so I admitted, "Not all of us were behind the plan to send Hara to Midnight."

"What brought you around?"

I doubted the question was even remotely casual, even if he appeared perfectly comfortable as he relaxed in one of the armchairs, leaving me standing awkwardly nearby.

"What . . ." I contemplated the question. Again, there was information this man might have, so I was honest *enough*. Jeshickah already knew about the prophecy, though she didn't believe in it, beyond its ability to manipulate people into doing things in her favor. "I'm familiar with your reputation. I'm sure you know the prophecy that Farrell was following from the day he bought me to the day he died. That prophecy said that Misha must take the throne. Whether or not it's true, it was Farrell's living goal and dying wish. The means may or may not have justified the ends, but they were the only means I knew."

"You sound like you have your doubts as to whether or not the prophecy will come true."

I shrugged. "I'm the one who said it, but I'm fallible, and falcon prophecies only show what *might* be, not what *must* be."

"But you still hope it's true."

"Of course I hope it's true," I whispered. Part of Jeshickah's arrogance was that she didn't care who spoke up against her as long as their actions didn't interfere with her empire, so I had no reason to lie. I wasn't telling Theron anything Midnight didn't already know, but for some reason the words made him smile.

He said, "And yet you're here."

"And yet I'm here," I repeated with a frustrated sigh. Theron had been a mercenary for hundreds of years. I wasn't going to trick him into saying anything he didn't already plan to tell me, so he might as well get to the point already. "And I don't know *why*, so if you wouldn't mind explaining—"

He cut me off with a raised hand reaching in my direction, and the words, "Come here."

Was that the only reason he had asked me in—because I had demonstrated that I was not averse to being a bleeder? Now that he was not obligated to be professional and controlled, now that it was sunrise and time to relax, he was willing to let down his guard.

No, that was too simple. If there was one thing I knew about Midnight's mercenaries, it was that they all put business before pleasure. Theron had chatted long enough to determine the extent of my value, information-wise, before he allowed himself to feed.

I could play that game, too. Maybe afterward, while Theron was lolling in the euphoria brought by taking my blood, I could ask him about Silver.

I went to where Theron was lounging comfortably in the plush armchair. He caught my wrist, and I thought for a moment that he would stop there, leaving me trying to stand while he bled me. Instead, he looked up with a chuckle and said, "I'm not looking for your blood right now."

I paused, replaying his words in my mind. Had I missed something?

The mercenary stood suddenly and I jumped to find him so close to me, his black eyes filling my vision.

"Your blood is delightful," he said, "and I would not

mind another taste sometime, but right now, I'm more interested in something else."

He wrapped a hand around the back of my head the same way he had when he had taken my blood earlier, but this time, instead of dropping his lips to my throat, he touched them to my mouth.

A heartbeat passed before I was able to turn my thoughts around to what had *actually* happened, as opposed to what I had expected, and then another passed while I tried to decide what I thought of this turn of events.

Theron was an attractive man. His hair was tied tightly back at that moment, but as soon as I tried I could envision him with that darkness framing his high cheekbones and oil-slick eyes. And his hands were strong but careful, as they trailed up my spine with just the fingertips touching me, barely a tease.

He broke the kiss and said, "If you want to leave, I will make no attempt to stop you. You're freeblood, and if you're willing to speak up against Midnight and support a queen on the throne whose reign you hope will topple that empire, you know what that means. In this case, I trust it means you know how to say no if you wish to."

I considered it. Throughout my life, touch had more often meant pain than pleasure. My own kind was too afraid of my magic and my reputation to even consider that I might have any interest in a lover.

It didn't take long to make my decision. I had done far more morally ambiguous things in my past than say yes when propositioned by an attractive mercenary.

"I have no intention of saying no," I replied. Maybe Theron was still hoping to get information from me. Maybe I would be able to learn something valuable from him. I kept both of those considerations in mind, but the heart of the matter at that moment was that it was good to be wanted, and held. I might lose everything fighting Midnight, but at least for now I didn't have to be alone.

CHAPTER 9

"YOU'RE AVIAN?" SHKEI *asked as Alasdair leaned against him.*

"Yes," she said, "I'm a hawk."

"Royalty?" he asked, trying not to sound as skeptical as he felt. It was hard to imagine any royal given to such a place, but there were no commoner hawks.

"Not anymore," she whispered. "How long have you been here?"

"It feels like forever." He held back the words that wanted to tumble from his mouth about the months that had gone by, often in darkness or hunger, while he was handed from one trainer to another without any sense of what would become of him. Instead, he asked, "When they brought you in, did you see my sister? She's a serpent, too, a white viper–" Alasdair tensed, and Shkei's imagination immediately conjured a dozen dark images. He asked

in a small voice, "Is she hurt? I don't know how long ago the trainer took her out of here. I haven't seen her since."

Alasdair asked softly, "Misha?"

"Yes, that's her, Misha." He was desperate for news, even if that news was bad.

"She's—" The hawk hesitated before saying, "I think I saw her before I was brought here. She was with a group of serpents. One looked like he might have been related to her. I heard them call another one Farrell."

Joy washed over him, along with relief. Somehow, Misha had made it out of this hell. He didn't resent the fact that she had left him behind; he didn't for an instant believe that she had any choice. If Farrell or Malachi had seen an opportunity to rescue either of them, they would have. They would come for Shkei, too, if they could.

I slept better than I had in months, grateful to revisit one of the few moments of near-contentment from Shkei's captivity, and one of the even scarcer comforts I was able to keep for myself: Shkei had trusted and forgiven me, even though I hadn't been able to save him.

Alasdair had done many kind things for my brother, but the greatest boon she had given him was ignorance. She let him talk about his family, and about home, and she never replied, *They were the ones who put me here.* She could have let him die hating us, but she had never spoken a word against his family.

I woke alone on the couch in the mercenary's sitting room. A quick survey of the room revealed my clothes, which some slave had apparently taken, cleaned, and returned in a neatly folded pile while I slept. I also helped myself to a platter of fruit, cheese, and fluffy rolls that were probably for me, since Midnight's slaves would never have left them out to get stale for Theron.

I couldn't resist poking around, but unsurprisingly, Theron did not keep any interesting papers or valuable information lying around the room. If there was anything worthwhile, it was hidden too carefully for me to find it without my search being blatantly obvious when he returned.

If he wanted me to stay and wait for him, he probably would have made that desire clear, so I let myself out. The clock in the hall told me it was almost noon, which was a little later than I had intended to start working on the task Misha had given me.

It would not have been a terribly long walk, but I didn't want to waste any more time, so I changed into my wings as soon as I was outside.

When people thought of Midnight, they thought of Midnight proper first. They thought of the famous gardens, black roses, and frescoes . . . and of course, they thought of the slaves. From the sky, though, Midnight's true power was even more apparent.

Down below, one could see the network of roads that

connected Midnight proper to the surrounding territories; the elaborate estates owned by Midnight's nobles; the village populated by the bloodtraitors who gave their labor to Midnight; and most importantly to me, the sprawling fields.

Many of the fields looked like they were currently in the process of being plowed or seeded, probably with the staples Midnight specialized in, such as corn, beans, and squash. A disturbing number already boasted stalks of wheat gracefully blowing in the breeze. I didn't know much about farming, but I suspected I had been right: it was already too late in the season for the serpiente to hope to clear, plow, and plant seeds for a real harvest this year.

I landed at the outskirts of the farmland anyway, hoping to offer my assistance, and was swiftly reminded of one inexorable fact of my existence: the vampires trusted me, but even serpiente who willingly worked for Midnight saw a half-falcon child of Obsidian and instantly became wary. I was able to get simple answers—wheat, for example, was first sown in the fall for an early-summer harvest, making it impossible for Misha to hope for a crop this year even if she could somehow acquire the seed—but the cool, suspicious looks the serpents here cast my way warned me not to try to woo allies too swiftly.

Maybe I wouldn't need to. Misha didn't know that Midnight would fall soon. When it did, these shapeshifters would be without masters, and their stores and crops would be available to those who needed them.

I offered my help anyway, if only so I could tell Misha I had. None of the serpiente wanted anything to do with me, but a group of avian farmers—ones blessedly unaware of the role my guild had played in Alasdair's sale to Midnight—were willing to let me bend my back to help with plowing and planting. I chattered amicably, but learned only a little about farming and less about my companions. Shapeshifters who came to Midnight did so because they couldn't go home. Some were guilty of worse crimes than the Obsidian guild had ever committed. They didn't ask me where I had come from or why I was there, and they didn't volunteer their own stories.

At sunset, I returned to Midnight, once again hoping to speak to Nathaniel. Unfortunately, he saw me first, scruffed me like an errant dog, and threw me so hard through one of the doors in the west wing that I hit the wall on the other side.

"Why do mercenaries all seem so anxious to drag me into their rooms?" I asked.

He responded by grabbing my arm and pulling me one room further, through an ominous wooden door I knew too well.

Though he worked as a mercenary, Nathaniel's room in Midnight was constructed like a trainer's, connected to a simple cell with slick stone walls and floor. The fact that his version of the cell boasted a thick area rug and a table and chairs did not stop my heart from pounding as he slammed the door shut behind us.

I hesitated to rise because the look on Nathaniel's face was cold and filled with warning. However, he did not immediately close the distance in any painful way, so I slowly found my way to my knees, and then back to my feet, watching him for a sign that he intended to strike me down again.

"Are you stupid or a traitor?" Nathaniel asked bluntly.

"Many people would say I'm both," I replied, trying to regain my equilibrium, and along with it the gentle pulse of my magic that essentially said to all around me, *Harmless, I'm harmless. I'm not worth your trouble. I'm quiet. Don't mind me here. Just let me pass by without bothering anyone.*

The magical wreath of complacency was my best defense. It was the reason I was able to come and go whenever I chose, rarely eliciting suspicion or even notice. It was why Gabriel had chosen to just throw me out when I had trespassed in his territory; he could have done far worse, and normally would have.

This time, though, Nathaniel replied by pushing me back against the cold stone wall with a forearm across my throat.

Given the impossibility of speaking aloud at that moment, I formed words in thought instead.

If you're concerned about where I spent my day, I said silently, guessing at the most likely reason for his fury, *I wasn't selling your secrets. I've given blood and flesh on the last day to keep one of the best mercenaries in Midnight from pursuing his suspicions too closely.* I let my hostility bleed into my thoughts. My time with Theron had been consensual and pleasant, and I would not object to another round someday, but it had been obvious that his interest was a combination of genuine attraction *and* the hope that I would let my guard down and reveal something valuable. The need to be cautious had diminished some of the fun.

The pressure on my windpipe lessened enough that I coughed, and then spoke aloud.

"Theron met with Jeshickah about some concerns he has regarding Kendra's line, and their potential interest in other leadership." I hoped he would respond by explaining, but Nathaniel remained mute, so I had to continue on my own. "Jeshickah thinks the possibility that any of her vampires would turn against her is absurd. But obviously you have, and Theron suspects others might. What I want to know is what this new empire would mean to the shapeshifters."

Nathaniel shook his head. "Nothing," he said. "There is another group of vampires, Silver's line, that claims to want to take control. They have been supporting my efforts . . . if *support* is the right word, since they seem to be a bunch of stuck-up ancient cowards as far as I can tell.

Either way, they are concerned only with our own kind so far. They say they have no interest in shapeshifters or witches, unless they meddle with vampire affairs."

So far. They say. Nathaniel didn't entirely trust Silver's line's answers, but he also didn't have any solid proof that they weren't sincere.

"If you've decided that I didn't share all your secrets with Theron," I asked, "would it be terribly inconvenient for you to take your hands off me?"

Nathaniel finally stepped back, letting me take a deep breath before I sat in one of the chairs and tried to conceal the sudden weakness in my legs. Vampires were a temperamental lot, and though my power helped me tamp down the worst of their fury at times, it made their occasional explosions even worse.

My power's ability to protect me was balanced by my knack to get myself into trouble, so I knew far too well how much I could heal, how quickly. I had feared another such lesson, but Nathaniel now seemed firmly in control of himself, no longer panicked that I had revealed his traitor's plan to Theron.

"I also heard Jaguar say something about acquiring a falcon," I said, rubbing my throat to ease the bruising there.

"You've heard a lot for someone who isn't supposed to be here," Nathaniel grumbled. "Ahnmik is having some kind of issue with an intended uprising, and wants to send a few of the ringleaders here to get rid of them. That's all I know so far, and more than you need to be involved in, given you are *supposed* to be with the Obsidian guild. I spoke to Vance, but all he knew was that Misha said you had gone to Midnight. He was not pleased, by the way. I gather he had his own plans before you disappeared."

I had guessed that Misha probably wouldn't tell the others the whole story. I briefly summarized my last conversation with my sister. When I was done, Nathaniel sighed before saying, "We'll work with what we have. In the meantime, I need you to get moving. The reason I went looking for you was because I need you at a meeting. Leave now, head into Shantel land, and bring this."

He flipped me a small, carved token. An intricate portrayal of the twisted roots and branches of a tree had been etched and burned into the surface of a wooden disc the size of a large coin.

"How many people are in on this?" I asked. The disc hummed with Shantel power, but did that mean Nathaniel had one Shantel witch on his side, or the entire civilization? Had he brought avians in on his plan, too? How many people could he possibly involve before someone slipped up?

Nathaniel elected not to answer. "You won't be able to fly over Shantel land," he said, "so you need to leave immediately by horseback if you want to arrive on time. Take one of mine; if anyone asks, I lent it to you because I want you back at the serpiente palace in time for the new queen's coronation, which looks like it will happen soon. No one will question why I want eyes on such a dramatic shift in power, and stopping in Shantel land will not take you so out of the way for anyone to question it."

"Misha won't like my returning before she calls for me," I pointed out. *As if she were ever planning to do so.*

Nathaniel shrugged dismissively. "Tell her Midnight sent you to spy on her."

It was a damning enough near-truth that Misha would believe it. Unfortunately, Aaron would, too, along with many others in our guild. That knowledge hurt more than I expected.

CHAPTER 10

SHKEI FELL ASLEEP *curled around Alasdair, and dreamed of basking in front of a crackling bonfire as his kin danced.*

He was jerked back to awareness as the trainer dragged him to his feet, nearly wrenching his arm out of its socket. He hadn't finished opening his eyes before he slammed into the far wall.

It was difficult to reconcile reality with his peaceful dream until he saw Alasdair's wide, golden eyes. Her fear had no place in the beauty he had briefly returned to in his sleep.

"Touch her again, snake, and I will peel the skin from your hands," the trainer said, his voice coldly furious. "Do you doubt me?"

"No," Shkei whispered.

When Gabriel turned toward Alasdair, she first cringed, and then stood, strengthening her shoulders, raising her chin, and deliberately stepping between the vampire and Shkei. The trainer smiled, but the expression spoke more of possession and anticipation than it did affection or pleasure.

My brother had trusted me implicitly, but in the end, I hadn't been there for him. I had watched through visions, unable to speak to Shkei or interfere in any way, while the hawk who should have hated us all had held him in the dark, comforted him, and tried to protect him.

I wished I could repay her, but all I could do for Alasdair or Shkei now was replay their memories in my head and try to make things right.

That thought spurred me on as I pushed myself and the horse beyond any sensible limits. This time of year, the days were long, and I used every moment, funneling magic into my mount when I otherwise would have needed to give her a break. I hoped to reach my destination early so I could get a sense of the area before Nathaniel—and, I assumed, others—arrived.

The days aren't just long, I thought as I rode. *It's the summer solstice.*

It had been exactly one year since Misha and Shkei had been taken. I wondered if the Obsidian guild would bother to celebrate Namir-da this year, or if they would ignore the holiest of serpiente holidays to avoid the painful memories associated with it.

Shortly before I entered Shantel land, I spotted the bright green tail of a quetzal out of the corner of my eye.

Vance alighted on my shoulder, and then shifted into human form, ending up behind me on the saddle.

"What's the news, and are we horse thieves now?" he asked.

"Even I'm not stupid enough to steal a horse from Midnight," I answered. "Jeshickah likes horses better than she likes people. Nathaniel lent me this one to get to his meeting, where I'm hoping he will finally explain his plan. Where's Kadee?"

"She stayed behind to keep an eye on Misha. She's a far better spy in the palace than I would be, and my wings were better suited to catching up with you. Where are we going?"

"Shantel land. That's all I know." I assumed the token Nathaniel had given me had some kind of power to guide me in the right direction, since even my magic couldn't help me navigate in the Shantel woods. "You don't weigh much, but we'll still be faster if you travel in your feathered form."

Vance nodded, and then changed shape again. The tiny emerald bird with a dramatic blood-crimson breast was able to ride comfortably on my shoulder, nestled under my hair in the crook of my neck, with his long tail feathers flittering behind.

He tucked his head down as if to sleep, and looked up with a squawk only once, when a powerful surge of magic rippled around us. The horse stomped the ground, resisting the reins long enough for me to be concerned before she relented and let herself be led forward. I only hoped I was leading us all well.

The sun was lost behind the trees when my ears popped and I was suddenly standing at the edge of a clearing. My attempt to hurry and arrive early had been foolish. Shantel magic had clearly created this place; Shantel magic ensured that everyone arrived exactly when they were supposed to.

I tethered the horse, Vance changed into human form beside me, and we stepped into the clearing. Darkness turned into heavy fog that further obscured the area. In the late twilight, I could barely see the shadows of others nearby. Magic veiled their identities more securely than the night did, so that even if I drew near, I knew I would have trouble making out their features.

I heard someone say sarcastically, "This is pretty," but when I turned the person who had spoken was nothing but a dark patch in the mist.

"Thank you all for coming," Nathaniel said. I was able to see him clearly, as if more light fell on him than on the others. "Several of you expressed a desire to remain anonymous for this meeting, and I have done my best to honor that request, so stop grumbling. In order to assuage other concerns, I would like to introduce one of our allies who is *not* afraid to show her face."

The mists shifted to reveal an elderly woman whose skin was the color of an acorn shell, except for streaks of milky white across her cheek, brow, and jaw. If I hadn't known better, I would have assumed they were scars, but I could sense the power around this woman. The pale stripes were what the Shantel called the "white curse," and they marked her as the famous sakkri, the witch who controlled the strongest of the Shantel's magic.

I knew which recent events had finally pushed the Shantel to participate in this rebellion. The sakkri's power was passed down from one generation to the next as the elder witch trained the younger, but the Shantel had been forced to sell the apprentice sakkri to Midnight just as she came fully into her power. What did they have left but to fight?

"We stand in a space between day and night, past and future, fixed and changeable." Though her body looked frail, as if she were at the end of her years, the sakkri's voice was strong. "The power of this place is designed to turn away anyone whose intentions do not align with ours and to reveal falsehoods, so I can vow that no one present tonight is here to betray us. The mist will hide anyone who wishes to stay secret, and only reveal those who choose to show their faces."

"That would be impressive. Should I believe it?" The question came from a man's voice with an accent I could not place.

His tone was more curious than challenging, but Nathaniel clenched his jaw, then took a moment to compose himself before turning to address the speaker, who was recognizable only as a vague outline.

"I am aware that you and your line have little experience with or interest in local cultures," Nathaniel replied, "but this would all go more smoothly if you would cease questioning my competence at every turn. You demanded to know who my allies were, whether they represented sufficient support for my plan to succeed, and how I expected to keep such a large plan secret long enough to pull it off. This meeting is your answer."

"It's rather naive to question a mercenary's methods," another voice remarked, teasing. All I could tell was that this one was female. "Not to mention rude. Nathaniel, is this your employer?"

"I'm simply a sponsor," the first voice replied.

Silver? I wondered. It would make sense that the vampire challenging Midnight for supremacy would be involved in Nathaniel's plan . . . but if he hadn't hired Nathaniel, who had?

"Fine," the first man said. For a man who claimed to be a "sponsor," not an employer, he seemed to have no compunctions about controlling the meeting. "Tell us who you've gathered, and what your plan is."

"As I said before," Nathaniel replied, "not everyone here is willing to share their names yet, but we have representatives from the Shantel, the Azteka, the shm'Ahnmik, Macht witches, Triste witches, the Obsidian guild, Kendra's line, and Katama's line—and you, of course, representing Silver's line."

"True," the sakkri whispered, tilting her head as if listening to distant music.

My skin crawled at the reference to the shm'Ahnmik, my father's people. Any purebred falcon who saw me would hate me on sight for being half serpent. My presence might be offensive enough for them to refuse to stay. Was their power strong enough to see past Shantel magic?

I suspected the uneasy murmuring I heard from the others was due to a different name in the list: Katama, Jeshickah's sister, who had sired the line that had created and ruled Midnight itself. Was Nathaniel referring to himself as a representative from that line? Or was one of the trainers in on this? If so, which one? The only name that came to mind was Gabriel, but though he regularly spoke up against Jeshickah, he seemed to enjoy the perks of his position too much to actively seek to destroy that empire.

As for the other groups listed, there were some I knew well, and others I only recognized in passing, such as Macht witches. I had heard Jeshickah refer to them as nuisances and vampire hunters, but I had never met any except failed assassins Jeshickah had already captured and broken.

"I still don't see why this needs to be so complicated."

This time, Nathaniel didn't bother to mask his irritation. He glared at the vampire from Silver's line.

"Midnight has existed, in one form or another, for over

five hundred years," Nathaniel said. "In my time, I have personally witnessed, heard about, or helped avert more assassination attempts than most of you can imagine."

When no one spoke up, he continued.

"In addition to the fact that Jeshickah and her trainers are all fierce fighters, Midnight proper is further protected by spellwork that limits what magic can be performed inside its walls, by shapeshifter guards, and by broken slaves who are trained fighters."

"Jeshickah or her sisters will be able to rebuild from anything other than—get this fog out of my face," a woman declared. "I don't care who knows I'm here."

The mist cleared to reveal an auburn-haired vampire I had never seen before. Nathaniel's representative from Kendra's line, perhaps? Some of them were strongly loyal to Midnight, but I had heard of others who had no interest in Jeshickah's empire.

"As I was saying," she said, tossing her head, "they will rebuild from anything other than complete destruction. The trainers would probably take over even if Jeshickah were gone; they don't know how to do anything different. And once they realize they're being targeted, the game is lost. So you need a way to take out Katama, Jeshickah, Acise, Gabriel, Jaguar, Taro, and Varick. And you need it to be fast enough that they can't fight back."

"What about people like Daryl?" Vance asked. "Or Theron? Midnight works with Kendra's line, too."

I winced, hoping I had been wrong about the vampire's lineage, but she grinned, and said, "That would be a very bad idea. Well, I wouldn't miss Daryl, but I'd have to object if anyone here somehow managed to harm Theron. And if you take Daryl, you'll need to take Brina. That would be child's play, until Kaleo came to avenge her, and if you killed him you would be back facing Theron."

Vance looked a little paler, but still had the nerve to say, "That's why most of us are anonymous, isn't it?"

"Safely anonymous, for now," someone else said—a woman, I thought, but I couldn't even tell that much for sure. "But everyone Nathaniel has brought in on this plan is by nature swift, intelligent, and deadly. *You* would not survive if any one of us were your enemy."

The way she emphasized the word *you* made me shudder, almost certain that speaker knew who Vance was. Either she could see past the sakkri's power, or Nathaniel had intentionally let her know who we were.

"True," the sakkri whispered again, "for you," she added, more softly. Vance wouldn't be a deadly enemy for anyone else in this circle.

"Thank you, Shevaun, for identifying our problem," Nathaniel said to the vampire from Kendra's line, as if he hadn't been interrupted. "Now—"

"But we have the advantage of numbers," another woman said. This time the mists revealed a blond-haired woman whose stance and toned form suggested that she was equally trained for combat. "Many of the fighters who guard Midnight used to be our kin. I refuse to believe that they would stand against us."

I didn't know the woman herself, but she had to be one of the Macht witches. Her resemblance to the broken creatures Jeshickah kept around or sold as fancy guard dogs was unmistakable.

Nathaniel sighed, as if he had heard this argument a thousand times.

"That misconception is going to get everyone involved in this plan killed," he said. I couldn't help but be amused by Nathaniel's frustration. He was clearly used to working with individuals who understood what it meant to be one of Midnight's mercenaries, who would give an assignment and an offer of payment and trust him to find the best way to carry it out. "Since I keep hearing it, I've arranged for a demonstration." Nathaniel held out a hand, and said, "Aislinn, come here."

The second-generation slave I had seen with Nathaniel in serpiente land suddenly appeared as if someone had drawn a curtain back. Her expression was serene—perfectly so, which meant she was probably terrified but subsuming her own emotions because her master had given her a command and she knew she needed to follow it.

"Aislinn here is a second-generation slave," Nathaniel said. "She was born and raised in Midnight, and thus is an excellent example of the people you are concerned about.

If anyone here can get her to disobey me, I will grant her freeblood status and let her go with whoever can offer her a happy and comfortable home. Who wants to try?"

"I'll test her, but I don't want to keep her." The man who spoke stood near Shevaun, but when the mists revealed him, it was clear he was no vampire. His silver-blue eyes could have passed for a falcon's if not for his bronze skin and dark hair, but the power seeping from him felt wrong for one of the shm'Ahnmik. Another kind of witch?

"She can come home with us," the blond Macht witch who had spoken about her kin in Midnight said without hesitation. "Aislinn, you wouldn't be a slave. You would be provided for, but free to make your own choices."

Now the slave *did* look frightened. The notion of slavery was nothing new to her, but to a second-generation slave, "freedom" was a myth. As was free will. I remembered that terror well from my first few weeks with Farrell and the Obsidian guild. If he hadn't bought me—and Jeshickah had let me live—this girl was what I would have become.

Nathaniel turned to Aislinn, and detailed the agreement to her. "What I want is for you to stand right where you are. That's all. Just stay there. If you choose to disobey me, you will not be harmed, or punished in any way. I will legally grant you freeblood status, and you may leave here with anyone you like. The good witch over there has already offered you a place to stay where I am sure she will take excellent care of you. Do you understand?"

The slave nodded, and said, "Yes, sir."

I didn't want to see what happened next. Unlike others in this circle, I did not need to be convinced. Many people believed Midnight's slaves obeyed out of fear of punishment, but it was deeper than that. Once the trainers were through with them, disobeying wouldn't even cross their minds as a possibility.

Nathaniel ceded the circle to the witch and the slave, and walked toward me and Vance.

"This meeting won't teach you two anything you don't already know," Nathaniel said, "but I do appreciate your coming." He looked calm, but I sensed his concern for the slave. He believed in the necessity of this demonstration, but he didn't like it either.

"This is your choice," Gabriel whispered to the young human man he had restrained against the slick marble wall. "I offered rest. You chose battle. I offered peace. You chose pain. I can make all this doubt and frustration and fear go away. You just need to let me."

"Who's the witch?" I asked, trying to distract myself from the vision and what was about to happen. I had seen trainers do this kind of thing to test a slave's obedience . . . or sometimes just for fun. Slaves learned that there was nothing they could do to stop or prevent pain. The only person who could take it away was their master.

"A Triste named Adjila," Nathaniel answered. "He's powerful for his age, and not squeamish, though unfortunately he isn't strong enough to go directly against Midnight's witches."

"Are there really falcons and Azteka here?" Vance asked.

"Of course," Nathaniel responded. "Shantel magic won't let me lie. But I will emphasize that I appreciate that you *both* made it."

In other words, there were no shm'Ahnmik or blood-witch magic users here—only us, providing the means for Nathaniel to stretch the truth and convince his allies and patron he had more power on his side than he actually did. My relief warred with disappointment. Any pure-blood shm'Ahnmik might want to kill me on sight, but without falcon or Azteka magic, what did we possibly hope to achieve?

Nathaniel winced at the same moment that a backlash of power and pain struck me. I looked up to find Aislinn swaying as thin strips of blood began to appear on her skin. The Triste's wordless, magical command was like a shove, and it made my skin crawl even though it was not directed at me. I bit my lip to keep from begging Nathaniel to stop this. It was too familiar.

I had never seen this happen to Shkei, thank the fates, but only because Alasdair had accepted the abuse on his behalf. Had Misha ever—

I tried to stop the question from forming fully in my mind, but with so much power in the air, my magic instantly brought the answer to me: *yes*, but not when she had belonged to him. She had let the trainer test her. It was the price he had demanded when Misha told him she wanted him to take Hara.

"This isn't *necessary*!" one of the others finally called, her voice cracking. "You've made your point."

Obligingly, Nathaniel said, "Aislinn, that's enough."

He reached out just in time to catch her as she collapsed like a puppet with cut strings. All that had been keeping her on her feet, I knew, was the power of his command.

"Heal her," Nathaniel said to the Triste.

"Naturally," he replied. "Impressive display."

Nathaniel just nodded sharply. "Rest, Aislinn," he said softly. "You did well. You did very well." Lifting his head to once again speak to the group, he said, "Any attempt to use Midnight's slaves against the trainers would have to start with tricking or manipulating them so powerfully that it overwhelms the training they have already been subjected to. I'm open to suggestions, but they need to be less stupid than the ones I've heard so far."

Resounding silence met his words. Even the vampire from Silver's line didn't challenge him again.

"Good," Nathaniel said after several seconds of silence. "We are finally on the same page. We will follow *my* plan. I will answer questions that need to be answered, but I will not respond to any more ridiculous demands for *proof*." He looked toward the vampire from Silver's line, who nodded. "The sakkri tells me her magic will be strongest on the fall equinox, so that is when we will move against Midnight. In the meantime, I will speak to each of you individually about your particular roles. For everyone's safety, no one here will be brought in on the whole plan until absolutely necessary. That limits the damage that can be done if any one person is found out. Now . . . go."

He turned around, and it was as if a bubble burst. I was familiar enough with Shantel magic that I was not surprised to find Vance and myself suddenly alone, nowhere near any visible clearing. The Azteka and falcons might have only been technically present because of Vance and me, but the Shantel had obviously put a great deal of magic into this plan already.

Would it be enough?

CHAPTER 11

"NO!" ALASDAIR PROTESTED, *standing up to the trainer as if he were not capable of breaking her in half with the smallest finger on his hand.*

With her golden hair soft around her, her skin pale but her voice solid, she somehow managed to seem as if she were looking down on the trainer, though he stood easily a head taller than her. She was slender as a willow, compared to a man who would have been strong even without the vampiric blood, so how did she manage to look so confident next to him?

"If he doesn't eat, then neither will I. How long do you think it will be before you have wasted your money on a skinny, sickly wastrel who holds no appeal for you whatsoever? How much will I be worth to you then?"

The trainer looked in her eyes. Surely he could see the resolve

*there. He knew this beautiful woman would starve herself to
death, if that was what it took to make her point.*

"Don't do this for me," Shkei whispered.

*She didn't understand. There were so many worse things the
trainer could do.*

*"I'll make you a deal, beautiful," the trainer said as he
ushered her out and shut the black door to the cell, leaving Shkei
alone once again, in the dark.*

A trainer's deal was never fair.

*"Don't do this for me," Shkei said again, to the darkness.
This courageous woman had set out to protect him. How could she
possibly believe she could protect* anyone *in this place?*

The only way to get the image of Aislinn's abused, bleeding, and unquestioningly obedient form from my mind was
to summon a vision of defiance.

Even in the vampire's cell, Alasdair had behaved the
way I had only ever imagined a queen was meant to. Instead of the cowardice and selfishness that I had seen most
royals exhibit, Alasdair had shown impossible courage.
Time and again, she had put herself between the trainer
and my brother, though no one would have blamed her for
protecting herself first.

Gabriel had crushed the regal woman who defended
Shkei, and left a docile slave referred to in Midnight's halls
as "Donovan's masterpiece."

I didn't know what Nathaniel's plan would cost, or

if I would survive it, but it would be worth it if we could stop the next Misha, Shkei, Alasdair, or Hara from being destroyed in one of those beautiful marble cells.

As my eyes cleared of the vision, I looked up to find Nathaniel standing nearby impatiently. "It isn't hard to see why Jeshickah found you frustrating," he said. "If you weren't so useful I'd give up on you, too."

I tried not to show how deeply that criticism bit. Would I ever stop feeling like I needed to prove myself?

"Why are there no serpiente involved in your plan?" I asked. "Or were they just hidden? Surely they would fight in your army. They have suffered as much as anyone under Midnight. I know you don't trust Misha, but I don't believe you couldn't find a way around her if you wanted to."

"The serpiente have a role to play," Nathaniel conceded. "It just isn't as fighters. They're my distraction. Midnight will be watching them closely. As long as Misha is in charge, your prophecy is in play, and Jeshickah has a reason to dismiss any rumors that reach her ears as big talk from naively optimistic shapeshifters who would never dare do more than gossip. I'm putting you in charge of making sure the serpiente don't go so far that Midnight feels the need to make an example of them."

"You don't believe the prophecy?" Vance asked, his voice curious yet neutral.

My heart nearly stopped as I waited to see if Nathaniel would betray my secret. "It's not my job to hang my hopes on a prophecy," the mercenary answered. "It's my job to ensure the outcome I've been paid to produce. I can use Malachi's prophecy to get the serpiente whispering and to convince some of my more useful allies that we have a chance in hell of succeeding, but that's all it is to me: a tool. So are you," he finished bluntly.

Vance flinched. "At least you're honest about it."

"Am I right that you were offered a place among the Azteka?" Nathaniel asked.

Vance nodded warily.

"The Shantel are powerful, but their magic is mostly defensive," Nathaniel said. "The Azteka, on the other hand, have some of the most powerful destructive magic users alive. I can't ask for their support because they won't talk to me. But they *will* talk to you."

"What kind of power *do* you actually have so far?" I asked.

"The Triste you saw today," Nathaniel answered, "and a handful of vampire hunters. They will all be useful, but it's not enough. Jeshickah has Tristes in her employ, and has invested a great deal of money into magical protections. We need to be able to unequivocally punch through those wards with our first shot, or else we won't get another."

"I don't know how to get to the Azteka homeland," Vance said.

"Start with the Azteka in the market," Nathaniel suggested. "You don't want to breathe a word of this in that place, but if you tell them you're interested in joining them they'll take you with them when they leave Midnight's land. Then you can ask them to join us."

Vance and I rode together to the edge of Shantel land, then he took the horse and some of Nathaniel's coins so he could drop the beast off at Midnight's market and start inquiring about the Azteka. "You'll tell Kadee where I am?" he asked, hesitating before we parted.

"I'll tell her everything," I assured him. Seeing the lingering worry in his eyes, I added, "If she's in any trouble, I will let you know."

"Can you still talk to me in my dreams?"

Vance's magic had once made that possible, but even then it had been an unreliable method of communication, and the greater self-awareness and wariness he had developed in the past few months had effectively locked me out. I might be able to spy on him if my magic cooperated, but I couldn't speak to him.

"No," I said, "but I'll find a way to contact you if I need to. Be safe."

"You too," he replied. "Watch out for Misha. I know she's your sister, but . . . she's not the same," he finished, after a hesitation. "Think about Nathaniel's demonstration when you see her."

Misha was nothing like Aislinn, superficially, but

Vance was right that her will wasn't entirely her own anymore. She hadn't been fully broken as a slave, but the trainer's half-done task made her more unpredictable.

Even if she hadn't been disturbed, I didn't want to see my sister become queen. I didn't want to see the fragmented remains of the Obsidian guild fall in around her as subjects. They wouldn't think of it as allowing themselves to be ruled, not at first, but it wouldn't take long before those Misha favored became the equivalent of courtiers, and any out of favor realized they either needed to grovel, or run.

"I will," I told Vance. I watched him mount the horse and start toward Midnight's market until he turned to look at me, as if feeling my stare on his back. Then at last I took my wings.

I wanted to run, and cursed Nathaniel for sending me back to Misha. I agreed that someone needed to help ensure the serpiente survived the three months between now and the equinox, but Misha had already sent me away once. It wouldn't take her long to find another excuse to get rid of me.

As I neared the palace, I saw two guards, squinting against my silhouette, nock arrows in their bows. I decided prudence was the better part of valor and ducked down into the trees to continue on foot.

It took all my willpower to deliberately walk toward

the guards instead of allowing myself to stop in the forest. I approached cautiously, ready to flee if they replied with violence. They greeted me coolly but respectfully, and made no attempt to restrain me. Instead, they explained that they had all been given my description and told that I was to have an honor guard if I visited. I doubted Misha intended much actual "honor," but even with my magic, directly countermanding the order would have raised suspicion.

Walking into the palace with a guard at each side still felt surreal. It was nearly time for the coronation, and we passed masses of other serpents on their way to the ceremony. The throng seemed quieter than it should have, but then, I had never stood amid those on their way to a royal event. Maybe they were always this subdued. The whispers I overheard made it clear the event had been announced and organized precipitously, probably as Aaron's common sense finally snapped under the pressure of Misha's magic. The crowd seemed evenly split between questioning Aaron's haste and praising him for stepping forward in their time of need.

Unfriendly, sidelong glances followed my progress.

Did you expect them to instantly love you? I asked myself, trying to keep an open mind, and not view the scene through the lens of fear. *You are still a white viper, and a falcon, and a member of Farrell Obsidian's guild. You're a bloodtraitor and a thief, and have worked with and harbored individuals guilty of high crimes. If they have any sense at all, they will never like you, never trust you.*

No one put an arrow or a knife in me, and I decided to be grateful for that.

I shuddered as my guards escorted me into the *synkal*, a room I knew all too well. The grand ritual room was where a king was crowned. It was also where trials, marking, and execution for high crimes occurred.

I reluctantly joined the crowd, who parted for me as if I might burn anyone I accidentally touched. Kadee came to my side and said, "You look . . . haggard. Where have you been? Where is Vance?"

I shrugged. There was so much I couldn't say here, with guards within arm's reach and a crowd around us anxiously waiting for their new king to declare his mate and take his crown. "I haven't slept much," I said. "Vance is safe. He's going to the Azteka."

Kadee bit her lip, probably thinking the same thing I was: she couldn't ask what she wanted to in this crowd. She nodded instead. "I guess I should have expected that." Her bland response conveyed no sense of loss or betrayal. She trusted that Vance hadn't left for good. "Most of the guild is staying in the Opal Hall, but I have a camp set up not far from the palace if you need a place to rest in the open air. I couldn't stand to sleep here after everything that happened to me."

I suspected that it was the soon-to-be queen rather than Kadee's memories of her time as a ward of the serpiente royal house that made sleeping in the palace difficult for her.

"Misha doesn't mind?"

"She . . . understands my reasons," Kadee answered, though I could tell she doubted Misha approved of them.

We had no more time to talk before one of the dancers called for the crowd's attention and Julian Cobriana strode onto the high dais with his son behind him. I had never witnessed a serpiente coronation, or expected to, so I waited against the back wall and tried to look politely interested instead of skin-crawlingly uncomfortable.

Julian's voice was distant as he formally presented Aaron to the crowd. He spoke a few words about Hara's sudden and devastating loss to Midnight, and how grateful he was that his son was prepared to step forward.

The king's eyes were glassy and his voice kept drifting off. A casual observer probably would have believed his words were weighed down by grief and despair over losing his daughter, but the swirling, tangled aura around him made it clear to me that his state was a result of magical and medical manipulation. He had been drugged in addition to being enchanted.

While Julian spoke, I watched Aaron. His outfit had clearly been put together with attention to the serpiente love of color symbolism. He declared his connection to the

Cobriana line in royal black: slacks that tucked into boots laced to just below the knees and an open-throated shirt of the same color. The snug vest he wore was likewise black, with a swirling decoration in white thread. The design was vaguely evocative of the letters of the old language, or a cobra's markings, but the color was clearly a nod to the Obsidian guild. Around his waist he wore two colored scarves, one the deep violet of mourning, and the other white embroidered with gold to represent the eternal tie to one's mate. Next to Julian's drooping, beaten shape, Aaron was a dramatic, determined figure.

Once it was Aaron's chance to speak, I straightened up, listening to his words while watching the crowd. He didn't have Misha's magic. Instead, he had the eloquence that is taught to the royal lines, and passion and dedication I recognized as his inheritance from his father—his *real* father, Farrell.

"Hara's loss is a wound that will not swiftly heal," Aaron said. Though his tone was subdued, his voice carried through the hall. "To you, she was a princess, soon-to-be queen. To me, she was all that and more. She was my older sister. She was the one I looked to as a role model and competed with as I grew up. She was the one who challenged and inspired me. She—" He stopped, and swallowed thickly. Real emotion, or another calculated pose? "I loved her, but her loss has made me realize that she was far from perfect. She made deals and compromises where she should have held a firm line. And in the end, she paid with her own freedom."

He let those vague, ominous words fall on the crowd, who shifted uncomfortably until he continued.

"I am a son of the royal house, soon to take the ser-piente throne, but what does that even *mean* when the royal line does nothing but dance like puppets on the end of a string manipulated by vile overlords? When we first settled here centuries ago, Midnight acted like benevolent shepherds, guiding lost stock to a safe barn. Since then, we have let them turn us into little more than sheep. We are animals that they control, fleece regularly, and slaughter when necessary. They claim to protect us, but what protec-tion is it really when they take our own flesh and blood whenever they feel we need to be taught a lesson?"

Again he paused, letting his audience consider those words, before he asserted, "No more. I refuse to be a sheep any longer. I refuse to grovel before a nation that flagrantly violates every sacred mandate that defines us as a people." I could see the tension building in the crowd as he made this bold—and dangerous—proclamation. Aaron lifted his voice to be heard over the low rumble of dissent. "I am not a fool. I have a plan, inspired by the woman who has helped me see what needs to be done . . . a woman *we* drove out, along with her kin, for the crime of daring to speak up against abuse and slavery that this royal house con-doned and even perpetuated in the name of obedience to

Midnight. Ladies and gentlemen, please allow me to introduce a woman with a lifetime of experience in making the sacrifices that are necessary to safeguard the freedom and dignity once granted to us by the goddess Anhamirak . . . my mate and your Naga, Misha Obsidian."

I was startled by the scattering of applause that greeted Aaron's announcement, and then became louder as Aaron held out his hand and my sister entered the synkal. She was flanked by guards whose eyes roamed the crowd cautiously, looking for anyone who seemed likely to start trouble for their new queen, but no one accosted her. I wondered how many influential serpiente she had privately met with in order to persuade them to give her this warm greeting.

I tried not to gag at the sight of my sister dressed, not as a child of Obsidian, but in a Cobriana-black gown. Her skin was pale with exhaustion and too much expended magic, but she shone with triumph as she climbed the dais next to her royal mate.

CHAPTER 12

"I DON'T WANT *to live this way."*

Shkei lay on the marble floor where he had fallen, too hurt and exhausted to even seek a more comfortable position. Alasdair knelt beside him, but the trainer hadn't left anything behind that she could use to do so much as wipe the blood from his face.

She took his hand–gently, because even that was bruised and swollen–and said, "I'm so sorry. This is my fault."

"Not your fault," Shkei managed to bite out. "His fault."

He tried to sit up but fell again, cursing. She caught him. His blood was already all over both of them, thick enough that her dress stuck to her skin where it had soaked through.

"Promise me," Shkei whispered. "If there is ever a chance, any chance, and you can get your hands on a knife–"

"No," she interrupted, body going cold, because she knew what he was asking.

She couldn't kill the trainer, but Shkei thought she could kill him. *Mercy killing was what the serpiente called it.*

"Please," *Shkei begged.* "I don't want to live this way. And I don't want him to keep using me against you."

Hara was in that cell now, sold into the very empire Aaron had just spoken so passionately against. As visions and memories of endless beatings passed before my eyes, my sister warmly thanked the serpiente people for welcoming her. As I recalled the look on Alasdair's face when we gave her to Acise, and the way Hara had gone ghostly pale when she saw Nathaniel, Misha simply and concisely explained her plan to fight Midnight as if she had not already acted against everything she said she stood for.

"Midnight is a system with rules," she asserted. "The vampires who run that empire pretend the rules are there for *our* benefit, but they are written so only Midnight itself can truly prosper through them. No matter what we do, instead of eventually earning our freedom, we inevitably end up in greater and greater debt, which we are forced to pay by selling Anhamirak's holy flesh and freedom into a land where slavery and abuse are as ubiquitous as air.

"Midnight has allowed the Obsidian guild's reputation to become as tarnished as it is because doing so has kept anyone from looking closely at how we survive. The Obsidian guild pays no tariffs to the vampires' empire. We accept nothing from them, and therefore we owe them nothing."

"Midnight has its own way of interpreting rules that don't work for them," a man in the crowd dared to assert.

Misha shook her head. "Midnight's creatures are immortals, and that makes them rigid. They will not want to violate their own laws. If we do not use their markets, buy their wares, or travel the roads on their lands, we will owe them no taxes. I won't attempt to deceive you—we will know lean times before we are truly independent. But we have always known hardship. It's easier to ignore when the things we sacrifice are slaves sent to Midnight and out of our sight . . . but it doesn't hurt us any less."

I stopped listening, slipped out, and waited for Misha and Aaron to summon me. They had both ignored my presence in the synkal, but they had to have noticed and wondered why I had returned from Midnight so soon.

It was nearly sunrise when I was escorted into the receiving room and told that the royal couple would be with me shortly. I waited awkwardly, trying not to make eye contact with any of the half-dozen guards, and fighting off any attempt my magic made to surface. At least one of the soldiers here had been present at my capture and marking when I was twelve—punished for being born the child of a white viper, and declared complicit with a murder we hadn't committed. I did not want to relive that experience now, from my point of view or theirs.

One of the other guards I couldn't help but notice was Jabari, who had been rumored to be Hara's potential mate.

His glassy-eyed expression made it clear that his participation was not entirely of his own will, but I did not think it was entirely due to magic either. The man moved stiffly, in a way I recognized from too many days spent inside Midnight's walls.

Was Misha practicing her skills at a trainer's art?

No, I told my magic. I did not want to see that either.

I wouldn't be able to resist my power's pull forever, I knew, but I hoped I would be able to hold it at bay until I was somewhere safer than this.

Misha had barely opened the door before she crooned, "Were my instructions unclear, Malachi? What are you doing back here?"

"They were clear," I answered. "But your plan was a bit too perfect. I did as you asked, but now that Midnight is convinced I am in their employ, they felt it was best to send me to watch *you.* I couldn't refuse without raising suspicion."

Misha looked as if she were about to continue haranguing me about my presence, but Aaron skipped that part of the conversation to ask directly, "What is Midnight saying about us?"

I considered what Nathaniel and Theron had said, and tried to decide what would be useful to share. "So far, they just seem curious to see what will happen next." Since I was supposed to be an acknowledged spy, I asked, "What do you want me to tell them about your plans here?"

"You can tell them the truth," Misha answered. "We're breaking no laws."

"Did you have a chance to speak to any of the farmers?" Aaron asked. Even with Misha's magic pushing him to actions and conclusions he otherwise wouldn't have considered, he was more focused on the plan and survival than on spiting at Midnight.

"A bit," I answered. I recapped the little I had learned about planting and harvest times, and watched Aaron's brows draw together. I could see the struggle within him as common sense fought the whisper of Misha's magic. He *knew* there was no way the serpiente could be self-sufficient in less than a season, but couldn't quite break free of Misha's determination.

If Midnight fell, the serpiente could claim a share of its crops, but Misha and Aaron didn't know that was a possibility.

"How are people responding to the new trade laws?" I asked.

"Not well," Aaron answered, sounding both frustrated and puzzled. Of course he was confused; he was too far out of his own right mind to understand why his people might not appreciate Misha's brilliant plan. Even Misha's magic couldn't control the entire serpiente people. "They don't like the idea of the royal house taking control of so much."

"If their freedom is so important to them," Misha said coldly, "they will soon realize that they were no *more* free under Midnight than they are now. If a peaceful economic protest doesn't suit them, they can pick up a weapon and fight."

Splash of blood, red on white.

Not now.

"If they try to fight Midnight, they will be slaughtered," I replied with a shudder. So that was Misha's plan. She knew the serpiente couldn't win against Midnight just by refusing to trade. She expected hunger, anger, and rebellion, and intended to funnel that fury into a hopeless battle.

With the exception of us two white vipers, serpiente had no magic. I had seen vampires run through with all sorts of weaponry made of every material, and I had never seen one fall. I didn't believe they were truly immortal . . . not really . . . but I did not think a serpiente army could possibly ever be equipped to stand up against Midnight.

The fall equinox was three months away. I understood now why Nathaniel was worried the serpiente might not survive that long.

"Midnight cannot just wipe us all out," Aaron argued. "If only we could get the other shapeshifter nations to join us, the vampires would *need* to recognize that they cannot control us all. They would need to back down, or risk a full-scale uprising that even they cannot quell."

"They don't need to control you all," I argued, "just a few of you." The possibilities danced behind my eyes, nearly blinding me. "You and Misha. A king here, a queen there, picked off. A young child of royal blood taken, raised like Vance was, in a rainbow-colored box."

"*You* all?" Misha snapped. "You're talking like you're not one of us, Malachi. Do you really believe that the people would all give up because one leader falls?"

"This is your choice," Gabriel whispered to the young human man he had restrained against the slick marble wall. "I offered rest. You chose battle. I offered peace. You chose pain. I can make all this doubt and frustration and fear go away. You just need to let me."

Huddled in the far corner, Misha watched the trainer work with horror . . . and envy.

Yes, *she wanted to say.* Please. Take away the ache of the constant cold, the grumble of hunger, the anxiety of waiting. Take away this knot of despair that chokes me as I imagine dying in this lonely place.

Sometimes he noticed her when he was bored, and those times would forever haunt her nightmares, but her white-viper magic kept her from ever becoming his primary focus. It kept her safe from that seductive offer: Give in, and all this pain will stop.

"You *want* them to take you back," I said, responding to the vision. The images had tried to force their way into my awareness earlier as I watched Aislinn, but I hadn't fully understood them then. Now I couldn't help the words that came out of my mouth as Misha's despair tried to drown me. "Some part of you realizes that you're nothing anymore, that you're hollow, and you're hoping that if you make enough of a fuss the vampires will get fed up with you and smack you down hard enough that you don't feel the pain anymore. Aaron at least *believes* what he's saying, that this is for the good of his people, but you don't. You're just doing this because you don't know what to do with yourself if you don't have someone to fight and someone to despise you."

I saw it coming, and I could have dodged, but I let the blow fall because she needed to hit *someone*. The punch was strong enough to send me stumbling to the side. Pain bloomed and I tasted blood in my mouth.

"Misha—"

She shoved Aaron back when he tried to protest.

"You are my *brother*!" she shouted at me. "Of all people, how could you ..." She trailed off, green eyes narrowed. "You don't understand."

"You're queen, Misha," I said, trying in vain to appeal to any spark of reason within her. "You could have so much power to do good, but you can't starve people until they raise up arms. They won't raise them against Midnight. They'll raise them against *you*."

"Why am I wasting my breath arguing with you?" she asked. "You used to go to Midnight as if you were on holiday. You can't handle being without a master for too long. Cradle to the coffin, isn't that the description they use for second-generation slaves?"

"This isn't necessary," Aaron tried to interject. "Neither of you means what you're saying. Misha, he's your brother. You don't want—"

"Guards, arrest him," Misha said, looking at me.

"On what *grounds*?" Aaron demanded, so startled he momentarily freed himself of Misha's magic.

"Treason."

I had expected her to hit me, scream at me, and probably throw me out of the building. I had not expected her to accuse me of a high crime and turn me over to the guards.

"Malachi Obsidian," she continued, "I love you as my brother, but I cannot continue to protect you." I anticipated where she was going only as those beautiful, soulless green eyes fell on my face once more. "You're a bloodtraitor and always have been. And you are under arrest for the abduction and murder of Hara Kiesha Cobriana."

I saw Aaron open his mouth to object, and shook my head at him. Anything he could say to defend me would just reveal his own guilt.

That didn't mean I intended to be taken and executed. I threw Aaron in front of the guards, and dodged my sister's clumsy attempt to grab me. I had almost made it to the door when I felt a strong hand close on my wrist. I pushed magic at those around me, but it wasn't enough.

Grabbed, dragged. Something hit me.

Gone.

Chapter 13

"PLEASE."

Alasdair knew that voice would reverberate in her dreams and nightmares forever.

Shkei, bleeding, broken, begging . . . and her with a knife near to hand. The trainer had left them alone, because he didn't believe she would ever do this.

He had made her do the work of hurting Shkei this time. He had assured her it would be worse if he did it, and so she had . . .

The memory, the thoughts, made her dry-heave.

And Shkei just said, "Please."

He had given her a weapon.

I can't.

But she also couldn't even say the words aloud, because the light was already gone from his eyes. In his mind, he had given *himself to the next world already; he did not want to live, not in this place, where he would only be used to hurt others.*

He had been so good to her . . .

She heard Master Gabriel finishing his conversation. He would be back in the room in moments. She only had another second.

"Please."

She held him close, and balled one hand in his hair to keep him still. She didn't trust herself to hit the heart with one blow, and wanted to make sure the end was quick, so she held the knife in a tight fist and drew it across his throat as firmly as she could.

The blood seemed to fly at first, as the last few beats of the heart drove it up into the air as if it would soar to freedom . . . but then it just gurgled, and finally slithered, out and down his skin.

She wasn't crying. The tears were gone.

There was nothing left as the trainer knelt beside her, took the knife from her hand, and said, "I'll let you dig the grave."

Alasdair had killed Shkei, and it had been a mercy, but it had broken her. She had given everything for my brother: her freedom, her pride, her soul, and finally the last bit of *self* she had, because Alasdair Shardae was not a murderer.

Alasdair Shardae could not dig a grave—even a shallow one, which was all she could manage in the frozen ground—and cover her last friend up with earth without even looking up at the sky. It had been the first time she had been allowed outside since she had been sold into that place, but the notion of escape never occurred to her.

Alasdair Shardae was not the one who had returned to the trainer's arms, after, and let him comfort her. That queen was gone. Only Ashley remained.

"Malachi."

I woke, shivering, in a serpiente cell.

This prison was quite unlike the one in which my brother had died. It was not even as nice as the one in which I had been born and lived for several years. In fact, it had a decidedly damp smell, and moisture settled into my skin from the dank, musty air. Whatever else one might say about them, at least Midnight's cells were dry and clean. I doubted this was out of mercy on anyone's part; Mistress Jeshickah was aware that human diseases spread quickly in poor conditions, and she wanted to maintain her property in good shape.

"Malachi Obsidian, Lady Misha is ready to speak to you."

The voice at the door was Jabari's. Blinking, I saw that he had two other guards behind him—too many for me to fight past. I would have to face Misha.

My own sister can't really want me dead.

Except she did. It was not healthy to challenge a madwoman's worldview, or to needle at the heart of that madness. If she had just wanted me out of the way for a while, she wouldn't have accused me of a crime with a death sentence.

I rose to my feet, feeling every ache and pain. Someone

had hit me after I was down, more than once, but I could walk. Jabari led me, not out, but deeper into the prison.

Serpiente did not believe in imprisonment as punishment, so this place was rarely used. Occasionally, criminals might spend a few days here while awaiting trial, if it was considered too dangerous to let them out, but the cells were never full . . . like they were now.

Hollow-eyed, shocked-looking serpents, some wearing the regalia of the royal guard, watched us pass on our way to the interrogation room. I wondered what crimes they were here for. Speaking up? It seemed that Misha had partly won the crowd through persuasion, but partly won her throne by removing those who would get in her way.

The interrogation room was normally a little better than the rest of the jail, because it included a vent high in the wall designed to bring fresh air into the room. My heart stopped when I saw Kadee, but then I realized she was alone and unchained. If anyone knew a way out of this place, it was the little half-human serpent who had once lived here.

Relief was quickly replaced by horror as I realized the room was not nearly as clean and sparse as I recalled it from my brief sojourn when I was twelve, with a table and lamp and a sideboard for water. A spike had been driven into the wall and shackles hung from it. One of the blade-tipped Obsidian staves sat nearby, and the sideboard held not a pitcher of water but a collection of weaponry, some bloodied. Misha did not take care of her toys as well as the trainers did.

How did I know they were Misha's?

I knew. She had brought the brutality home with her. What else did she know how to do anymore, when faced with opposition? The sweet voice of reason was no longer whispering in her ear.

Jabari regained my attention by shaking me fiercely, clacking my teeth together before I braced myself and focused on him.

"Where. Is. Hara?" he demanded.

"Is Misha coming?" I asked.

He shook his head, sharply, before saying, "Not today, but the guards outside your cell don't know that. I'll let you go with Kadee, but only if you answer my question. What happened to my mate?"

Kadee would have told him already if she thought it was a good idea, so I paused to imagine what would happen next if I replied with the truth.

I could tell Jabari that Misha and Aaron had conspired to sell Hara. He would get the word out, if he could work quickly enough to keep Misha from stopping him. Hara would become a rallying point, until the people overthrew Misha. She would become a symbol of their revolt. The serpiente would not take up arms against the vampires to prevent starvation, that I believed, but if Misha spread her madness through the people, filled the jails, and practiced a trainer's art on her chosen few and then they learned Hara was alive . . . they might go for Midnight. With torches and pitchforks and bows and a few blades, serpents better suited to shepherding or selling handmade jewelry in the market would attack Midnight's stronghold.

And they would be slaughtered.

I dropped my gaze, and put every ounce of power into forcing him to believe me.

"Hara is dead," I said. The backlash of agony, the last rattling breath of dying hope, nearly took my voice away. "I didn't do it. None of us did. It was a stupid accident, in the river." Was I making any sense? Not really. There were plenty of rivers where plenty of people had met their demise trying to cross, but the heir to the throne would not have been so foolish. It didn't matter, as long as Jabari believed the key facts long enough for me to get out—Hara was dead, and I didn't do it. "Misha saw it as an opportunity." He could and probably would rethink it later; *believe me for now!*

Jabari nodded.

"We need to get out of here," Kadee said, her gaze shifting nervously between me and Jabari. Hara's lover felt too strongly about the cobra to be swayed for long even by magic, and I didn't have the time or imagination to come up with a better lie that he would believe once I was out of sight.

"How?" I asked Kadee.

"Change shape, follow me." She hesitated before saying, "I'm hoping you're not much bigger than I am. Can you ..." She waved a hand vaguely at Jabari.

I could push at his mind so that he would "see" us go a different direction than we went. Even if his loyalty to Misha was questionable, we did not need a royal guard to know all our secrets.

Kadee and I both changed shape, and slithered down into what must have been some kind of rodent burrow. Kadee was right that it was a snug fit; if I did not have her assurance that there was a light at the end of this tunnel, I never would have entered it, because it would be impossible to turn around if we hit a dead end.

We emerged in one of the small, cramped caves that Kadee and Shkei had once extensively explored. I wondered how they had found this particular passage, but put the thought from my head. I didn't want to think about my brother right then.

I didn't want to think about anything at all.

"I don't think Misha knows where my camp is," Kadee explained as she led the way, "but if you could work some of your magic to ensure that, it would help me sleep more easily."

"I can do that," I said as I surveyed the area. The site, a nearly enclosed hollow set between a fallen tangle of scrub and some large boulders, had been well chosen for concealment. Serpiente guards might have walked by this spot even before I added a few enchantments to make it less noticeable.

We prepared for dinner. Kadee had acquired quality supplies from the palace while those doors had been open to her, and the ground had finally dried enough to allow a fire, so the food was plentiful and delicious, but neither of us was in the mood to appreciate it.

I finally told her the details of Nathaniel's plans, and that Vance had gone to speak to the bloodwitches among the Azteka.

"We lost Aika," Kadee reported when I was done.

"What do you mean, *lost*?" I asked.

"She told me last night that she trusts Misha more than she trusts Nathaniel. She's backing the new serpiente royal house. She says she won't tell Misha about our plan with Nathaniel."

What would Misha do if she heard? Would she want to join us? No, she would never be willing to work with Nathaniel, and he had made it clear he didn't intend to work with her.

"We have to trust her," I said. "I can see why she is more comfortable siding with Misha than with a mercenary. I don't think she would do anything to undermine Nathaniel's plan, even if she doubts it will amount to anything."

"What about us?" Kadee asked.

"I'll have to go back to Midnight," I said, making my

decision as I spoke, "to try to convince them to wait to deal with the serpiente until after the fall equinox." That was the task Nathaniel had charged me with. If I couldn't do it from within the serpiente palace, I would have to work from the other side. "If Misha and her crew can avoid repercussions from the vampires until then, the serpiente will survive after Midnight falls."

"In theory, they aren't breaking any laws," Kadee said, "so it should be easy enough to persuade the vampires to . . . not ignore it, precisely, but allow the serpiente to destroy themselves." She sighed, and stared into the distance. "While you're at Midnight, I'll go to the Shantel. They will know the best way for me to help." Before I had any chance to agree or disagree, she whispered fiercely, "It feels so wrong to separate this way. You at Midnight, Vance with the Azteka, me with the Shantel. You're all the family I have left."

I took her hand, and her cool fingers clenched around mine.

"Tomorrow we go our separate ways, but we're still on the same side," I assured her. "If we live through this, we *will* be a family again. Don't forget that."

Don't forget me, I thought, desperately, because we were each going back to the nations that had once welcomed us. The Azteka would let Vance join them, and if they did, he would have a rank near to that of royalty; he was not trained, but even without the skill to use it, a bloodwitch had holiness in his veins. Kadee had been brought by the Shantel from human land to the serpiente, and they had always kept their arms open to her.

After Kadee fell asleep next to the flickering fire, I stayed up for a while, just watching her and trying to imagine a world where a fifteen-year-old girl didn't need to face so much.

I couldn't.

We were so few now. Everyone in my blood-family was gone. Shkei lay in a shallow ditch in Midnight's land. I would not make the mistake of seeing Misha as my sister again, not when I knew she was willing to make me a scapegoat as soon as I became an inconvenience. Farrell was dead.

Kadee, Vance, and I were the last of the Obsidian guild.

A slow fury kindled in me.

By whatever gods might ever have been, if we were the last of Maeve's kin, then we would fight every last inch to honor everything the Obsidian guild had ever stood for.

We were a people who bowed to no master, who chose neither to rule nor to serve, but who would strike as vipers at a tyrant. We would bring down Midnight, and then if need be we would bring down the serpiente royal house, until we could face our own shadows again without guilt, and shame, and fear.

CHAPTER 14

"JUST *GO*!" MISHA'S *voice cried out, causing several of the Obsidian guild to turn their heads in concern. When they saw that Malachi was with Misha, they turned away again. "Just go and leave me alone," she whimpered, collapsing in front of the fire and pulling her knees to her chest. "I look at you and you're like a stranger. I can't stand it."*

Malachi stood, speechless. There had always been a bond between them, forged in a white-viper's power, but that connection had been damaged by abuse, and was now frayed and weak.

She turned her back and dragged herself into her tent, seeking solitude.

"Our brother is dead," he whispered, too quietly for her to hear.

He needed to get away, before he demanded more from her

than she was capable of giving and broke the last threads of love that connected them.

Maybe Midnight will let me have the body, *he thought.* A corpse can't be worth that much to them.

If nothing else, maybe the Obsidian guild could give Shkei a proper goodbye, with a pyre in the woods and his ashes scattered to the wild winds.

Malachi was nearly at Midnight proper when he remembered what the trainer had said: I'll let you dig the grave. *Gabriel intended to use Shkei's body as yet another object lesson for his hawk.*

As the sky darkened and sleet started to fall, making it impossible for even his powerful wings to hold him aloft, he sought refuge in Brina di'Birgetta's greenhouse.

Wishful thinking and willful blindness had kept me from anticipating that Misha would betray me. She hadn't been able to stand the sight of me since she returned from Midnight. Even if I hadn't stupidly spoken up and argued with her, she would have turned on me eventually. I was too much of a reminder of the past.

I was still charged with trying to protect the serpiente people, though. By the time I reached Midnight a few minutes before sunrise I had a vague idea of a plan.

I sought not Nathaniel, but Theron. He did not always spend a lot of time in Midnight, but I hoped that the conflict I had heard of between Midnight and Kendra's line would have kept him close. If he was still here, I could find a way to drop the information about the serpiente in a way that would lead Midnight's decision-makers to the conclusion I wanted. After all, he was a mercenary; information was power. I could pretend to be shocked and numbed by my sister's betrayal, a lost soul seeking comfort.

I wasn't fooling anyone, and I was the only one I was having the conversation with. I *was* shocked. I *was* numb. I *did* want comfort.

I knocked on Theron's door, and heard him stir inside.

He opened the door with an amused expression, and said, "Malachi, come in."

The door closed behind me, making a dull *thunk* instead of the usual resounding, nearly resonate *click*. But perhaps that dullness was in my own mind. Everything seemed muffled.

"Are you in there, Malachi?" Theron asked, sounding a bit less amused than he had initially looked. He was a mercenary, not a nursemaid. He would turn me away if he was expected to simply comfort me.

"Misha had me arrested for treason," I said, making no effort to keep the emotion from my voice. I was a good liar when I needed to be, but I didn't want to test my skills against someone with Theron's reputation. "She accused me of kidnapping and murdering Hara."

"Ironic," Theron replied. "But—"

I didn't let him continue. The words needed to get out

before he threw me out. "She and Aaron have this whole elaborate plan to stand up to Midnight. They're mad." Theron hesitated, listening. "They'll destroy themselves," I asserted. "Midnight won't even need to step in. Misha thinks the serpiente will stand up against Midnight, but they won't. They will go after the royal house. If they take Misha, I think Aaron will return to his senses, but they're more likely to go after the Diente—"

"Slow down," Theron interrupted. "Start at the beginning."

I looked up at him, and shook my head. "I didn't come here to cry to you. I thought—"

He caught my wrist when I reached for him. Business before pleasure, always.

"Start at the beginning, Malachi, and we will see what we can do about sparing your sister's life. That is what you want, isn't it?"

Isn't it? But . . . "No," I said softly. Honestly. "It's too late. I'm sure everyone here knew it was too late before Gabriel sold her back to us. I just don't want her to bring the entire serpiente people down with her."

It occurred to me at last that, if Misha and Aaron were both killed, only Julian Cobriana would remain. I did not want to imagine what his fury would look like when he unleashed it against the survivors of the Obsidian guild.

"Aaron would be a fine Diente," I said. "Misha is the problem."

This wasn't the direction I wanted this conversation to go. Midnight was surely capable of getting rid of Misha, but Nathaniel needed her on the throne in order for his plans to work. Even beyond his intention of using the serpiente as a distraction, the last thing we needed was for Midnight to give another brutal example of what happened when someone was foolish enough to stand up to them just as Nathaniel was gathering his allies.

"What is Misha's plan?" Theron asked.

There, that was the question I wanted. I answered as well as I could, explaining about their scheme to rebel against Midnight by acting within the pure letter of Midnight's law.

"Huh," Theron said at last. He leaned back against the wall, looking amused. "Things do come full circle, don't they?"

"I don't understand."

"Farrell never told you?" he asked. "Of all the people in your guild, I had thought that Farrell would have been honest with *you*."

"Told me what?"

"The deal he made," Theron said, "to buy you and your mother. She was a strong woman, a good worker. Jeshickah did not get rid of her lightly."

A lead weight settled into the pit of my stomach, and I asked, "What was the deal?"

"A bit over two decades ago, the serpiente queen came

up with a plan to stand up against Midnight by working within the letter of Midnight's laws. She was on the verge of making an alliance with the avians and Shantel, as well. Jeshickah did not want the royal leaders involved to become martyrs, so she arranged for their destruction. Discreetly. Farrell agreed to take care of the Naga."

My tongue seemed stuck to the roof of my sandpaper mouth, so it took me three tries to whisper, "Lady Elise?"

Theron nodded.

Lady Elise, Hara's mother, Diente Julian's previous queen.

"As I understand it, Farrell's mate left him because she disapproved of the arrangement he had made based on a child's prophecy."

Melissa, Aaron's mother. It all fell into place like a shattering mirror, sending shards of glass every which way, each one accusative, showing me my own traitor self from a hundred angles. The crime we had spent so many years denying . . . Farrell *had* done it. I wanted to doubt it, but what Theron said made too much sense.

If I hadn't spoken, made up that prophecy, Farrell never would have made such a damning deal and left so much ruin behind him. Of course, Midnight probably would have found another dupe—

No, I was done thinking that way.

But I was a child! I was seven, and all I wanted was not to die. How could I be blamed? It wasn't my fault . . .

I looked up at Theron, and suspected that whether or not he could read my mind, he knew every agonized thought running through my head.

"You are sure," he asked, "that taking Misha would be sufficient?"

I nodded, numbly, and then realized what I was doing and said, "I don't think it will even be necessary. Once winter sets in, the serpiente will revolt. Serpents don't like to go hungry. You just need to wait a few months."

"Should we attempt to save Aaron, then?"

I shuddered. Would it have worked, Elise's plan? She had two other nations on her side, a crucial step that Misha and Aaron had ignored.

"You won't be able to manipulate Julian after all this," I answered, "so you need Aaron. That's how you pick who gets to rule, isn't it? Who will play your games and be your quiet little doll?"

Theron just shrugged, and said gently, "Frightened little snake."

He reached for me and I went to him, as grateful for his touch as I had ever been for sunlight after a long, dark night, or a hot meal after days without so much as a dry biscuit. I wasn't thinking about manipulating him anymore, though part of my mind was aware that I was supposed to be careful, supposed to make sure I was saying the right things.

To hell with Lady Elise or Midnight. Would *Farrell* still

be alive, if I had not convinced him I was some kind of prophet and Misha a future queen and savior? He probably would be. He would have raised Aaron as his own son.

The Obsidian guild, led by Farrell and Melissa, still would have lived on the fringes of serpiente society, but they never would have become the hunted, hated outlaws we had made them. Treason; murder; Melissa had accused Farrell of rape when she left him, probably because she needed a severe enough excuse to abandon him, but could not directly accuse him of Lady Elise's murder without implicating herself. Both charges carried a death sentence.

I had spent most of my life hating the royal house for what I considered their unjustified, vicious persecution of our guild, and now realized it was my betrayal—not theirs—that had put an ax over the heads of everyone I loved and claimed to care about.

Would I get Vance and Kadee killed next? They still believed in me.

"It will be taken care of," Theron assured me, before his fangs pierced my throat.

I threw myself into the swift-flowing current of his mind more desperately than I ever had. I didn't want to return. I also knew Theron wasn't the type to want to keep me. He wasn't one of the trainers; he didn't keep pets or sycophants around. He was interested in my information, my flesh, and my blood.

But he let me sleep there, which was good, because

I did not know where else to go except back to the cells where I had begun, before I spoke those foolish, selfish words.

Someday, my sister, you will be queen. When you and your king rule, you will bow to no one. And this place, this Midnight, will burn to ash.

I made it all up like a child's fancy, then walked across the bodies of the dead in order to get from that day to this one.

Nathaniel had said we needed to fulfill the first half of the prophecy in order to give the others hope that the rest could someday come true. If we could turn my lie into reality, would Farrell's death be worth it? Would I be redeemed?

This place will burn to ash.

Chapter 15

ASHLEY PULLED THE *soft woolen shawl more snugly around her shoulders as a cold draft slipped into the main room from the back cell. The slave who stepped through the heavy back door was quiet and unafraid; he had come to clean the tomblike room, and had no reason to fear the trainer's wrath as long as he performed his task well.*

Master Gabriel had just returned to his desk when three sharp raps at the door made him look up with annoyance, as he had every time he had been interrupted while trying to read and respond to the stack of letters and invoices currently in front of him.

Each time, Ashley had watched him anxiously as she tried to decide if there was something else she should be doing, and then been relieved as she realized he would tell her if he wanted her. Until then, like the slave in the cell, she knew her place. She

returned to her journal, where charcoal and inks portrayed scenes
she couldn't quite recall.

"Enter," Master Gabriel snapped, his voice like a thunder
crack as the last of his patience eroded and he shoved himself to
his feet. If it was Mistress Jeshickah on the other side of the door,
or someone else capable of protecting him- or herself, the trainer's
irritation would move to the next convenient target as soon as the
unwanted conversation was done. If it was anyone else . . .

But Master Gabriel's glare became a grin when he saw
who had just walked through the door: a slender woman with
snow-white hair, mist-green eyes, and an expression of haughty
defiance.

She raised her gaze fearlessly to his–

Then stumbled, flinching, as he closed the door behind her
with an ominous click.

"Misha," Master Gabriel purred. "You must need something
very badly if you are willing to come to me *for it."*

The last time I had slept in Theron's rooms, I had woken feeling more peaceful than I had in years. This time, I
rolled out of bed and to the floor, struggling to pull myself
out of "Ashley's" mind before I could see the rest of that
scene.

Misha had gone to Gabriel to arrange for Hara's sale.
I knew, just as the trainer would have, that he was the
only one capable of giving her the perfect revenge she desired . . . which meant when he decided he was in the

mood to play, she didn't have any other options. I had seen the bruises when she returned to our camp afterward. I didn't need to watch them be created.

I splashed water on my face, but passed by the provided breakfast with a shudder. Alasdair had been so beautiful, so powerful and vibrant and passionate. To see her reduced to someone whose single motivation was watching that creature's every little twitch as she awaited his orders was almost as disgusting as being forced to watch Misha "bargain" for the privilege of giving him a cobra princess would have been.

That wasn't all.

I paused in the middle of reaching for my shirt, as I reconsidered what I had seen. In particular, I thought about the journal. What did a broken slave have to write about? She hadn't been writing something dictated by the vampire. She was recording her own thoughts and memories. Was that possible? I had never met a broken slave with the independent thought required for such a task. On the other hand, I remembered the strange tremble of power I had felt the last time I saw the hawk.

Something was left of her.

I resolved to see her again when I had a chance, if only to assuage my own curiosity. I would need to wait until Gabriel was out of the building, but that happened often enough, since he had properties and businesses he managed outside Midnight. I needed to stay nearby anyway, in order to keep an ear out and try to manage Midnight's response to the serpiente. I could also keep making contacts among the farmers in the village; every ally I had there would help ease the transition after Midnight fell.

In order to accomplish all that, I had to avoid getting kicked out. That meant I needed to make myself useful. I didn't know enough about farming to make that my primary occupation for the next three months, so my choices were the same tasks I had accepted during my many visits over the years.

One option was to claim a space in the dormitory that housed the regular bleeders. Though the household slaves might be bled on occasion, they needed to maintain enough strength to perform their day-to-day duties, so Jeshickah maintained stock specifically for the vampires' meals. Those slaves tended to be physically lovely and mentally vacuous. Jeshickah herself might not be fond of my looks, but she knew my blood was valuable. If I put myself in that group, she would not object. It would even give Nathaniel a convenient way to seek me when he needed to do so.

Given what I knew of his reputed preferences, it would also cause Theron to lose all interest in me. That could be useful if I felt his information-seeking became dangerous, but it would also cut him off as a means of funneling information and suggestions to Jeshickah.

The next best choice was the infirmary. My magic

was no good for healing others, but I had a steady hand, a working knowledge of herbs and poultices, an intuitive sense of what was wrong with a sick or injured human, and most importantly, a strong stomach.

So many people came and went each day that the infirmary was an excellent place from which to keep track of all the major happenings in the building. It also provided ample opportunities for someone to discreetly make contact, which Nathaniel did a few hours after I started working there.

When I reached his rooms with the salves and herbs he had requested, I was startled to discover another second-generation slave huddled on his floor, trembling in fear and pain.

"It's not serious," Nathaniel said as I froze, unsure if I was supposed to go to him or to her. "Give the supplies to Aislinn. She can take care of her friend while we talk."

I handed salves, bandages, and warm water to Aislinn, who accepted them with a lowered gaze and a murmured, "Thank you."

"I didn't beat her," Nathaniel snapped, when I still hesitated to follow him. "That distinction belongs to Daryl. Aislinn brought her back here afterward and asked me to take care of her. It seemed a convenient way to make her happy while also giving me an excuse to see you."

I nodded, and tried to put the abused slave out of my mind. At least Nathaniel's ulterior motive meant she was being taken care of better than she would have been if Daryl had been left to see to it.

I had more trouble ignoring the rest of his explanation. "Aislinn *asked* you to take care of her?"

Nathaniel nodded distractedly. "The primary trait that makes a second-generation slave more valuable than a broken first generation is their ability to take initiative and think flexibly. It makes them better able to predict their masters' needs. It also means they occasionally show moments of genuine compassion for their fellow human beings. It got Aislinn in trouble the day I bought her; she stepped up to defend one of the other kitchen slaves."

His gaze drifted over to where Aislinn was washing blood from the other slave's face, and his brows tensed in a frown.

Too quietly to carry to the two slaves, I asked, "If this is common in second-generation slaves, can we use them in the attack?"

Nathaniel started as if I had poked him with a knife, and then shook his head. "Aislinn made it further than most, probably because she's so bright, but it's a trait Jeshickah watches for. If I hadn't bought Aislinn when I did, she would have spent the last couple of weeks in a trainer's care."

"But you've ignored it?"

"I've *nurtured* it," Nathaniel answered. "I've rewarded

her every time I've seen her show any initiative. I'm going to end up spending an absurd amount of money on that girl over there to keep her out of Daryl's hands, and I have no idea what I'll do with her after that, but it's another support that will help Aislinn do what I need her to do on the equinox."

"Which is?"

Nathaniel hesitated, as if just realizing how close he was to divulging his plan to me . . . and then he sighed. "I suppose you need to know, since I'm hoping you can help." Voice sharper, he added, "It's the only choice, since you obviously aren't suitable as a spy in the serpiente palace. How is it that you can walk the halls of Midnight without issue, but can't keep yourself out of trouble with your own sister for more than a *day*?"

I bit back my immediate, defensive response, and settled on the absolute truth. "Jeshickah doesn't see me as a threat."

Nathaniel considered the words, then nodded. "You're too much of a mirror to Misha."

"Have you heard from Theron this evening?" I asked, turning the conversation away from my fractious relationship with my royal sibling.

"I heard bits and pieces," he answered. "I gather he is encouraging Jeshickah to wait before interfering with the serpiente. Your doing?"

I nodded, and briefly relayed what I had told the other mercenary.

"Be careful with Theron," Nathaniel warned at the end. "He isn't an idiot, and I'm sure he knows you're trying to manipulate him. He'll allow it as long as what you're saying is in Midnight's best interests, but he will turn on you fast if he catches you in a lie. So far he believes your only motivations are to protect the serpiente and yourself from Misha, but if he senses more is going on, he won't hesitate to use either charm or violence to learn what."

"I understand." He had already found a way to weaken the foundation of my world with just a few words, which I now sought to confirm. "Was Farrell really hired to murder Elise Cobriana?"

"Yes, and Jeshickah was quite pleased with the outcome," Nathaniel answered. "The serpiente believed it the work of an outlaw, but the Shantel and avians recognized it for what it was and backed down . . . at least for a while. Additional measures were taken later when the other queens looked like they might reconsider."

I had always wondered how the Shantel queen could possibly have been lost in a hunting accident in her own forest. As for the avian queen, it was well known that she had suffered some form of affliction for years now, something serious enough that her daughter Miriam had taken the throne at a rather young age. *That* illness was assumed to be Midnight's retaliation for something. It was exactly the kind of example Nathaniel didn't want made of Misha and Aaron while he was trying to gather allies.

I didn't need to know any more. "What do you want me to help Aislinn with?"

"I'm still working on how to arrange the attack itself," Nathaniel explained, "but one thing I've decided is that I will need a distraction. I want to make sure Jeshickah and the trainers are too occupied to fight back until it's too late. The only thing I can think of that would engage all of them would be some kind of major disruption among the slaves in the south wing."

"Like a fight?" I asked, trying to imagine what it would take to get all five trainers involved.

"Like a riot," Nathaniel said. "If I tell Aislinn to start something, she will, but she won't get far trying to convince other slaves to act up. Can your magic help?"

I could hide the Obsidian guild camp from serpiente guards, and convince trainers to let me walk out of a room without a beating—most of the time. Could I get broken slaves to fight their masters, even for a few minutes?

"If one or two slaves act out, a trainer restrains them and throws them in a cell until they can figure out why," I pointed out. "Broken and bred slaves are too valuable to damage unnecessarily. But if there is enough trouble that they all need to be there to subdue it, the trainers will start killing."

Nathaniel nodded. Clearly choosing his words with

care, he asked, "What do you think will happen to the slaves once Midnight falls?"

"They ..." I trailed off. The Shantel had a standing policy to execute escaped slaves on sight. Would that continue after Midnight fell? All the shapeshifters would be facing scarce food and other resources this winter. They might take in broken slaves who had once been their own kin, but they wouldn't offer the same charity to humans with whom they had no blood-ties.

"You have the Shantel as a resource, if you can use them discreetly," Nathaniel said, taking my silence for acceptance. "They might be able to provide some kind of illusion or drug or—I don't know. Magic isn't my field."

"So, you're planning a distraction," I said. "What about the rest? Do you have *any* idea yet how you're going to make the attack itself work?"

Nathaniel nodded again, slowly. I didn't like the expression on his face.

"Fire," Nathaniel answered. "The prophecy says this place ends in fire, doesn't it?"

I scowled at the vague response. "Do you *have* a plan?" I knew he had lied about having stronger allies than he actually had. I couldn't remember exactly how he had phrased his statement about his grand plan—had he avoided the Shantel's truth magic then, too?

"Do you remember what Shevaun said when Vance asked about killing Theron?" Nathaniel asked.

I nodded. The vampire at Nathaniel's big meeting had made it clear that she would avenge Theron. "What's his relationship to her?"

"He's the one who changed her," Nathaniel answered. "They used to be lovers. Most of the vampiric community is like that. Everyone has allies who would be willing to raze heaven and hell to avenge particular deaths. *Everyone.* And no matter what precautions we take, given sufficient motivation, anyone who sought revenge would be able to divine our identities." He paused to let me consider that statement. When the trainers were dying, Jeshickah had for a while blamed the Obsidian guild; she had promised to break every member of the guild and turn Aaron into the first of her new trainers if we did not break the spell. If she died, her sisters, Acise and Katama, would probably be just as vicious with their retribution.

"You wouldn't have taken the job if you thought it was a suicide mission," I said. I was willing to die if necessary to destroy Midnight, but I doubted the mercenary was so self-sacrificing. He had to have a plan.

"The assignment I accepted was to destroy Midnight, and leave a path for Silver's line to take over," Nathaniel said. "They plan to end the slave trade, among other things. I wasn't actually hired to kill anyone."

"Then how—" *What do you think will happen to the slaves once Midnight falls?* The demonstration with Aislinn hadn't been intended to convince people Midnight's slaves wouldn't help us. It had been done to show people we couldn't help *them*. "You can't kill the vampires, so you mean to destroy the . . . the *property*." I spit out the last word. Such a bloodless, passionless way of describing people.

"You know they wouldn't survive Midnight's fall anyway," Nathaniel argued. "Broken slaves, second-generation slaves, *need* their masters. We can't save them."

"You really think Jeshickah will give up just because you kill a few slaves?" I could have been one of the children Nathaniel was talking about slaughtering. Shkei. Alasdair. *Misha.* The last thought rocked me because it supported what Nathaniel was trying to say: it was too late to save them.

"We only need to weaken Jeshickah long enough for Silver's line to step in and take over. And I'm not talking about 'a few slaves,'" Nathaniel answered. "If we can gather a strong enough force, and distract the trainers long enough, we can gut Midnight. Every private home and property, every market and field Midnight owns, even—"

"*No.*" He could convince me to accept the slaves' deaths because I had grown up in Midnight. I recognized that as necessary, though I wished I were naive enough to dream otherwise, but Nathaniel's plan would hurt more than slaves. "Take the vampires' property. Fine. Brina's greenhouse, Jeshickah's mansion, Taro's estate, all of them. I will help you slaughter all the innocent, broken souls you intend to sacrifice if I must. But don't touch the blood-traitors' village or the market."

"They're all parts of Midnight's economy," Nathaniel argued. "If—"

"If you want my cooperation, you will promise me, on your reputation as a businessman, that you will leave the village and the market. Otherwise you won't just be leveling Midnight. You'll destroy the shapeshifters, too."

The look in his eye was cool, calculating. The serpiente and avians were clearly acceptable losses in his eyes.

"If I disappear, Vance and Kadee will question you," I said, before he could decide I had just become a liability. "Vance is your link to the Azteka and Kadee has the ear of the Shantel. You can't risk alienating them. Besides, leaving the fields and market will make the shapeshifters stronger. Maybe they can stand up to Jeshickah if she tries to rebuild."

Nathaniel let out a frustrated sigh, and finally extended his hand, saying, "Fine. I will leave the fields and market intact. And you will turn your power toward helping me create a sufficient distraction while I find a way to burn this place to the ground."

I reached out and shook his hand. It was foolish to trust a mercenary's honesty or kindness, but one could always trust them to hold to a business deal. "Fire won't burn stone," I answered, thinking of my own prophecy in the face of Midnight proper's granite and marble walls—and then frowned, because I had heard those words before. Not personally, but . . . *Kadee.*

"You look like you've thought of something."

"When Midnight was threatening the Shantel, one of its witches created a spell he said could burn even the magically protected Shantel forest." Kadee and Vance hadn't shared all the details of their adventures with the rest of our guild, but I had overheard her describing that particular threat to Farrell. "In the same conversation, he tried to barter for some of Vance's blood. He said he could use it to make a fire that would burn stone."

After I spoke, I realized that Vance might not like my offering his blood up as a possible solution to our problem, but it was too late to take it back.

Nathaniel looked intrigued, but not overly optimistic. "I know the witch you're talking about. He's centuries older than Jeshickah, and has spent all that time working on his craft. I only wish I had someone with his level of power on my side, but he's far too enamored with Jeshickah's empire for me to risk approaching him. Adjila and the hunters have some power, but unless Vance can get a bloodwitch to join us, I think we're limited to knives and torches."

We had three months. I had been given the daunting

task of instigating a slave riot. Nathaniel needed to find a way to burn stone. And I needed to accept that the price of our success would be the death of every man, woman, and child who had the bad fortune to be dragged into Midnight's walls.

CHAPTER 16

"YOU'RE STALLING," MISTRESS Jeshickah accused. *"We both know you could have finished with the cobra and moved on by now if you wanted to. Instead you're wasting time."*

"It's my time to waste," Master Gabriel replied. His voice was calm, but Ashley could see the tension that always ran through his frame when he argued with* her.

"You've been neglecting—"

"Don't forget, Jeshickah," he interrupted sharply, *"I am your employee, not your slave. I'm the best you have, and—"*

"Arrogant wretch."

"—you know it. You also know that, unlike your other trainers, I could walk away. So don't push me."

Mistress Jeshickah scoffed. *"Where would you go?"* she challenged him. *"Silver's little town in the hills, where ownership* means nothing and your profession is outlawed? The first thing they would do is steal your little hawk, just to prove they could."

"What makes you think I need a master?" As he spoke, he instinctively reached behind himself, wrapping an arm around Ashley's waist and pulling her protectively against his side. "I own land in a dozen different countries, and can live quite comfortably on the income from my trading enterprises."

"You could survive," the Mistress of Midnight allowed. Her cold gaze settled on Ashley, heavy with speculation. "But you couldn't live, not without the work you do best."

The weeks that followed seemed to pass in agonizing slowness. Midnight harvested its first round of wheat and planted a second, and other crops were flourishing, while the serpiente struggled to even start trying to do the same. Misha's approach to discipline and control made the task harder, since she kept accusing her would-be farmers of sedition. Her paranoia was obvious to everyone but Aaron, which was bad for the serpiente people in the short term, but at least made it easy to continue to convince Midnight that they didn't need to step in.

Meanwhile, in the six weeks since I had come back to Midnight, I had become half convinced that Gabriel was either directly involved with Nathaniel's plot, or else aware of it. He seemed focused on challenging Jeshickah at every turn, had refused multiple offers to sell Ashley, and though he was certainly spending some time working on Hara, Jeshickah wasn't the only one who had noticed his lack of focus on that project. Did he know Midnight's time was coming to an end, or had he always been this way?

As for me, I had managed to see Ashley a handful of times in the infirmary as she picked up materials, and was almost sure there was part of her left intact. Perhaps Gabriel's waning interest in his career as a trainer had begun early enough that he had neglected those last few strands?

If any of her soul remained, I knew I wouldn't be able to let her burn at Midnight's end.

Finally, I heard a rumor that Gabriel would be out of the building for the next two nights. I counted down the hours before my intended visit.

"What do you see, when your gaze goes distant like that?"

I gasped at the feel of cool breath behind my ear. I had thought Theron was asleep, as I lay in his arms and let my visions wander among all the threads I was trying to keep track of in Midnight and among the serpiente.

"The cells beneath the serpiente palace," I answered. It wasn't entirely a lie. I had been there earlier. "They're always full these days."

"So I've heard," Theron answered. "Taro has been given the task of finding jobs for all the serpents who've come to Midnight to flee Misha. Most of them are willing to take work previously done by the most menial slaves in exchange for protection from their own royal house." He idly tickled the skin over my collarbone, and added, "You're lucky you came here early, or you would never have been allowed to stay in Midnight proper."

"It's almost time to balance accounts. Do you know what Jeshickah plans to do if no one appears?"

Every four months, Midnight collected all the money shapeshifter nations owed to them for food, resources, and tariffs. In two weeks, when accounts were due, Jeshickah would have to decide whether to agree that the serpiente owed her nothing, or to attempt to collect whatever she felt she deserved. That would be the most dangerous time for the serpiente.

"As you predicted, the serpiente are already crumbling from the inside," Theron replied. "Jeshickah is prepared to agree that the serpiente accounts are in good standing at the moment, in anticipation of charging a premium when they come begging for resources this winter."

It was impossible to conceal how much of a relief it was to officially hear those words. Theron chuckled as my entire body relaxed, and remarked, "You are strangely protective of a group that has reviled and shunned you all your life."

"I don't care about most of them." I *did* care, more than I liked to admit, but it was easier to convince Theron that my motives were more personal. "But I owe it to Farrell to keep his son safe if I can, and Aika and Torquil were always good to me."

I hadn't seen Vance since Nathaniel had sent him to speak to the Azteka. Occasionally my magic let me know he was alive, but the bloodwitches he was with were blocking my vision from telling me more. Kadee was still with the Shantel; from that vantage, she probably knew more about Nathaniel's plans for the attack than I did. I had personally proposed a dozen possible options for triggering the riot Nathaniel wanted, and the Shantel had declared all of them beyond their ability. What we needed was precise and potent, but Shantel magic weakened drastically outside their forest.

"I need to work," Theron said regretfully, pulling away from me with a stretch. I rolled over lazily as he walked out as if I had no plans to go anywhere. But as soon as I was confident he wouldn't see me, I dressed and hurried to Gabriel's rooms.

The door from the hall was not locked. After all, who would be crazy enough to come here without permission . . . except, of course, me?

I found Ashley at the desk in the trainer's bedroom, leaning over a journal, sketching. I watched her, hypnotized by the focus in those golden eyes.

If anyone else had intruded, she probably would have looked up, expecting her master, but my white-viper's blood gave me the chance to observe her. Though I could not read her book from where I stood, I could see that there were words beside her drawing.

Words indicated thoughts, self-awareness, beyond what a truly broken slave should possess.

I drifted closer, consciously trying to hold myself outside her awareness, but when I leaned over to read the words on the page my hair fell across my shoulder and brushed her cheek. She jumped, slamming the sketchbook closed at the same moment that she stood and pulled away from me, wedging herself between the wall and the desk with an expression of fear.

That, too, made no sense if she were as broken as everyone said. Slaves were afraid constantly, but they rarely let that fear influence their behavior.

"I'm not going to hurt you." Deliberately, wondering how she would respond, I added, "Alasdair."

Her eyes widened further, and met mine directly as she said, "I know you."

My heart leapt. Did she remember what I had done to her, or did she simply recognize Malachi, Mistress Jeshickah's pet mongrel falcon, who had visited her a few weeks ago?

"I know you, as well," I answered. I reached for the sketchbook, slowly, giving her a chance to tell me not to . . . but of course she didn't. I wasn't a vampire, but I wasn't a slave, and unless her master had given her specific orders regarding what she should do with me, she wouldn't get in my way.

Opening the book made it clear that she wasn't recording anything Gabriel would have asked of her. Instead, I found snippets of poetry from the avian court, along with innumerable sketches. Many showed the trainer, but there were also graceful forms with wings, and images of the land as a painted tapestry, the way it looks to a bird flying above, where rivers become ribbons and thousands of trees blur together to look like a soft cushion. She used no color, but the black strokes revealed details from her mind she surely didn't dare share anywhere else.

Some pages showed faces—some even labeled with names. These were hazy recollections in smudged charcoal, as if she had been unsatisfied with her ability to re-create them . . . or perhaps frustrated that she had even tried. One of the clearest made my breath catch. Shkei's face was blurred, as if Alasdair had intentionally smudged out the lines of his cheeks and chin and brow, but his eyes and mouth were clear enough for me to feel as if I was staring directly at my brother.

"Do you remember him?" I asked.

"No." The answer was too abrupt. Part of her did. She didn't want to.

"Alasdair . . . if you want, I can take you away from here," I said. A suicidal, impulsive offer, but even if it meant risking everything—Nathaniel's plan, the fall of

Midnight, my own life—I would have followed through with it if she said, "Yes."

Instead, she said, "No, you can't."

"Do you want to leave here?" I asked.

She was bent, but some part of her was unbroken. How else could she put these images on a page? If I could get her away from the trainer, surely I could find that core of her soul that he had somehow missed—or intentionally left behind? People said the trainer Gabriel loved his slave.

Whether or not that was true, he would surely destroy someone who dared to steal her.

But she answered, "No. Please leave."

The request only solidified my certainty that she could be saved. A broken slave didn't make demands unless very clearly instructed to.

If I tried to take her out now, without a better plan, she would fight me. On the other hand, I had it on good authority that Midnight would be gone in less than two months.

Was I repeating the same mistakes that I had made with Misha? I just knew that abandoning Alasdair when Midnight fell would be like abandoning my brother all over again.

I backed away, saying only, "As you wish." As long as I was checking on old sins, however, I wanted to look in on Hara, who had to be in the marble cell connected to the back of this room. The door was closed, and certainly locked, but the heavy black key hung next to it. "I just need to—"

"No." She caught my wrist as I reached for the key.

"No?" I asked.

She didn't flinch this time. Instead, she said, "Master Gabriel left instructions. That door must remain locked."

She would be certain, and assertive, in response to his commands.

"Is Hara in there?" I asked.

The hawk nodded. Quietly, she added, "If you unlock the door, she will probably kill you."

Was that a warning, or did I detect a hint of protectiveness in her soft voice? Did she know me, *really* know me, and know that I was Shkei's brother?

Or did she know that I was the villain who had sold her to the trainer in the first place?

I couldn't concentrate on either possibility without going mad. Instead, I thought about Hara, who needed to remain behind a locked door. That meant the trainer thought she would run, which meant she wasn't broken. Yet.

My glimpses of Gabriel's ongoing conflict with Jeshickah had shown me the truth—Gabriel had put off working with her, either because he had other projects he found more interesting, or because he was deliberately baiting Mistress Jeshickah.

Or perhaps he was utilizing a more subtle strategy?

A trainer who wasn't in a hurry could still erode the will of a captive over time, even if he didn't dedicate his energy to finalizing the destruction. Misha and Shkei had been in that situation; their white-viper blood had kept them from ever being the center of attention, but it hadn't been sufficient to stave off the daily cruelty—or occasional kindness—that could chip away at even the strongest will.

CHAPTER 17

"I KNOW YOU."

Ashley tried to ignore the cobra when she spoke. She had been ordered to tend the newcomer's wounds, nothing else. She didn't even want to look into the woman's eyes.

"Alasdair."

That name. How she hated that name now! It brought nothing but memories of pain, guilt, and self-loathing.

"Don't you remember me?" Why did people keep asking that? "We've spoken a dozen times," the woman insisted. "Just last fall, we talked for an hour about my mate, Jabari, and your search for an—"

"Stop it!" Ashley hissed, looking up at the serpent's jewel-bright eyes. "I'm not that woman anymore. I don't want to talk about her."

Instead of relenting, the cobra's gaze widened with triumph.

"Do broken slaves often want things?" she asked. "You remember who you were. Admit it."

"If I admit it, will you be quiet?"

The cobra tilted her head as she considered, and then winced as if the movement hurt. "If you remember who you are, why do you stay here?" Hara asked. "Why do you let him do this to you?"

Hara was a shapeshifter. She wouldn't die of her wounds or get an infection.

Master Gabriel would understand.

Ashley walked out, and locked the door behind her.

As I contemplated Hara's situation and Alasdair's state, I realized the serpiente princess had seen the same things I had. She had been just as certain as I was that "Ashley" wasn't all that was left of the hawk princess.

Now, how was I supposed to get her out of Midnight before the fire came?

I shoved that thought aside as I stepped back into the living room, only to find Jaguar seated with his feet up on the coffee table, looking directly at me.

"It's funny," the trainer said, never taking his eyes off my frozen form, "but when Gabriel asked me to check in on his cobra while he was gone, he neglected to mention that you might drop by."

I needed a good excuse, and I needed it immediately.

Nothing came to mind.

Think, Malachi!

Jaguar stood, and pushed past me as he walked into the bedroom. For an instant I thought I had been miraculously dismissed, but when I tried to slink away he grabbed me by the hair and dragged me after him. I caught his hand in mine, but I couldn't do anything to escape.

Fighting my way out wouldn't be wise even if I could. All the white-viper magic in the world would not keep a trainer from catching me if I tried to run. That was their nature. Even if he didn't intend to harm me yet, he would be forced to make a point if I challenged him.

My heart nearly stopped when he asked Ashley, "Are you all right?"

If she told him what I had said, I was a dead man. No, worse than a dead man. Dead men couldn't feel pain.

"I am fine," the hawk answered. Was it just wishful thinking that I perceived dislike in her clipped, careful voice? There was no way for me to know her motivation, only that she did not volunteer more of an answer. Hopefully the trainer would refrain from asking anything like, "What did he say to you?"

Still bringing me with him, Jaguar reached to the black key I had been interested in not long ago. This time, Ashley did not speak up; either he had permission to be back there, or she knew better than to argue with a trainer. As for me, I absolutely did not want to follow Jaguar into that horrific place, but there was no way to escape unless he released me.

He let me go once we were across the threshold. In Jeshickah's disturbing style, the floors were exotic marble, polished smooth, lovely unless you had personal experience to tell you they looked just as beautiful with an added splash of red.

Too many memories distracted me at first, keeping me from tracking Jaguar as he crossed the cell and cautiously approached a figure hunched in the far corner.

I knew from my brother that these cells were cold, even in summer. That chill could sap the energy from a serpent, who relied on heat in the air to warm the body.

Hara Kiesha Cobriana lifted her head groggily and stared at Jaguar for a long time, as if unsure where she was or who he was . . . or who she was? I didn't know. Was this a fugue left by the trainer's work, or just too much time without warmth and proper rest? This cell was not cold enough to kill her, and unlike a human, a shapeshifter couldn't get sick, which meant keeping her here like this would make her docile without endangering her life.

I wasn't sure what Jaguar was looking for, but he didn't wait for Hara to fully rouse before he turned and led us both back out. I heard Hara call after us as we left, but already the heavy door was closing, locking her away again.

"What were you after, Malachi?" Jaguar asked me,

now that he had established that both of Gabriel's valu-able pets were accounted for.

"I don't know," I answered.

The response earned me a backhand that sent me stumbling into the wall. What was I supposed to have said? *I came here to kidnap Master Gabriel's beloved hawk,* seemed like a bad idea. *I don't know* sounded stupid, but at least that was in line with what most of the trainers expected from me.

Jaguar had known me when I was a child, unable to understand simple commands or speak in anything but nonsensical garbage. If I held to the wide-eyed line of *I don't know,* he would believe me. Eventually.

Unfortunately, he didn't keep talking to *me*. He asked Ashley, "What did he do when he came in?"

She didn't know me, or owe me any loyalty. In fact, if she had known me, she would have owed me only hatred for the part I played in bringing her here. So I could not feel betrayed when she said, "He spoke to me, and then he tried to open the cell door. When I told him Master's orders, he left."

A concise explanation that did not include the worst transgressions.

"What did he say to you?"

There it was. Could I convince Jaguar that I just wanted to see how she would react? Saying you could help a slave escape was not the same as *doing* it. They could and certainly *would* hurt me for it, but I hadn't actually taken or damaged any property.

"He said that he would not hurt me, and that he knew me."

For some insane, merciful reason, she stopped there. My heart nearly stopped with her.

"That's all?" Jaguar pressed.

"Yes, sir."

Wide, golden eyes looked right at him as she spoke. *Lied*, to a trainer's face. Lied cleanly, calmly, convincingly.

Jaguar turned and stared at me as if trying to divine answers in my face. He knew something was wrong. Maybe he believed I had bewitched the hawk. I knew I hadn't, but that seemed more believable than that a supposedly broken slave had lied to a trainer for me.

Worse, Jaguar was obviously in the mood to work. Was his falcon boring him? Frustrating him? Did she need some time to cool down, or recover? Either way, he was considering taking his mood out on me. I was freeblood, but I had given him an excuse.

He was too focused for my magic to help me escape. If I ran, he would catch me, and if I fought, I would lose. There was only one way out of this that didn't involve a trip to the infirmary.

I didn't attempt to meet the trainer's steady gaze. Doing so would be like locking eyes with a wolf—an indisputable challenge. Instead, I broke eye contact and dropped to my knees, bowing my head.

The self-protective action was instinctive, encouraged by the ghosts of a thousand slaves who had lived in this building before now. It was only as my knees hit the floor that I imagined what Farrell would say if he saw me like this. For years, I had kept my two selves separate—the Malachi who lived by the code of the Obsidian guild, and the Malachi who came to Midnight to lose himself for a little while. By and large, when I was at Midnight I didn't act as a slave, addressing every vampire and shapeshifter with a title and kneeling whenever one of my "betters" approached, but I did what I needed to survive.

Like this.

I shifted my weight, preparing to stand and accept the consequences of defiance, and every muscle in my body seemed to lock. Fear became a physical thing, holding me down and warning me what would happen if I went through with this.

You'll lose your usefulness to Nathaniel, that cowardly part of me whispered. *Pretend a little longer, and you can stay here. Cause trouble, and where will you go next?*

I let out a yelp as someone pulled me awkwardly to my feet.

"I need to borrow this one."

Nathaniel's voice was one of the sweetest sounds I had

ever heard, though it wasn't louder than the hateful internal voice that was calling me six different kinds of traitor to everyone who had ever loved, trusted, or respected me.

"Did you send him in here?" Jaguar asked.

Nathaniel laughed. "No. But who knows why Malachi does anything?" I managed to get my feet under me, but didn't fight Nathaniel's bruising grip on my arm. He was saving my skin. "How's *your* new falcon faring?"

I didn't understand the conversational change immediately, but Jaguar apparently did. He nodded, and said, "I never should have accepted another one after Charis. I understand now why Jeshickah decided outside stock might improve them. Has Daryl made a decision?"

"That's why I was looking for you," Nathaniel replied. "He rescheduled our first meeting. Do you mind if I hold on to Charis for another night?"

"Better you than me," Jaguar scoffed. "I told Alain I would deal with these two traitors, and then I'm not taking any more. They're not worth it."

"I'll keep that in mind next time Ahnmik approaches me," Nathaniel said. "Come, Malachi."

He dropped my arm as he turned away, and I followed gratefully, asking no questions while Jaguar could still hear us.

As we passed through the front door and into the outside air, Nathaniel hissed, "You are damn lucky I was there. What the hell were you doing, Malachi?" I hadn't even opened my mouth before he continued. "Never mind. It's time for you to return to your own kind. I'm sure Kadee will be anxious to see you."

His shove seemed intended to propel me into the air with its force alone. I changed shape and awkwardly made it into the sky, screeching in protest once in falcon form because I knew better than to protest with human words where Midnight's guards could overhear us. The message was clear enough, anyway. Kadee was with the Shantel. That was where Nathaniel wanted me to go. Had they come up with a plan for the riot Nathaniel wanted to trigger?

I made the mistake of flying directly into Shantel land, hoping their magic wouldn't reject me. I ended up on the ground with my head spinning and my stomach rolling. I was still struggling to see straight when a leopard loped into sight. My eyes watered at the way the guard's knife glistened when he changed back into human form.

"I think I'm expected?" I managed to say. "Malachi Obsidian. I—" I almost said, *I'm working with Nathaniel,* then realized at the last moment that it was unlikely that every Shantel knew what was going on. That would be far too many people to trust. "I'm a friend of Kadee's. And I think the sakkri wants to see me."

"Think?" the guard repeated skeptically.

"The message wasn't entirely clear," I admitted. "But I'm supposed to be here."

He sheathed the knife, though I knew better than to

take that as a sign that he trusted me. If I tried to cause trouble, the forest itself would come to the guard's aid. "This way," he said, turning his back on me confidently to lead the way. "Does this have anything to do with the other falcon?"

"Other . . . falcon?" Nathaniel had talked about borrowing Jaguar's project, Charis. Was she here? Was she on our side?

Did Nathaniel realize I was probably the *last* person he should be relying on to negotiate with a falcon? Considering how my father's people thought of mongrels like me, I would be safer with Jaguar.

I don't know what you're thinking, Nathaniel, but it isn't a good idea.

CHAPTER 18

"YOU ARE HARA *Kiesha Cobriana," Ashley murmured to the lethargic serpent. "You are heir to the serpiente throne. You are one of the strongest women I ever met."*

Ashley's memories of the days before she came to this place were faded and blurry, but Hara's needling these past weeks had brought a few things into focus. Ashley had no interest in remembering who she used to be, but she knew who Hara was supposed to be, and couldn't stand to see her so cowed.

The serpent's eyelashes fluttered, but her eyes didn't quite open. "Leave me alone."

Ashley looked instinctively at the door, though she knew Master Gabriel wouldn't be back for hours.

"Hara Kiesha Cobriana," she tried again, using the name like a magical spell to draw the cobra back to herself. "If you—"

"What is the point?" Hara snarled, finally looking up. "It's

been weeks. My father isn't coming for me. Either Nathaniel didn't tell him I'm here, or Midnight wouldn't let him buy me out, but he isn't coming."

"*That's the only reason you were fighting?*" Ashley asked. "*You were waiting for someone to rescue you?*"

She was hoping to get a rise out of the other woman. Hara's glare was halfhearted, but it was something.

"*What right do you have to criticize?*" Hara challenged. "*You let him treat you like a pet. You deny even remembering you were once Alasdair.*"

Every time I caught a glimpse of Hara with Alasdair, I wanted to hate her more, but ended up hating her a little less instead. I wanted to be angry that Alasdair was supporting the woman who had sold Shkei into slavery, but after each vision ended, I had to admit I admired how Hara—even while fighting tooth and nail to retain any semblance of self—was still pushing "Ashley" to admit who she had once been.

Had the falcon Jaguar worked with held on to who she was? He had expressed frustration with her and her kind, so she had clearly given him some trouble, but he wouldn't normally work with Nathaniel to sell her unless he felt she was ready to serve. It didn't seem like a trainer to give up on a project.

My head was spinning with possibilities—some good,

and some very bad—as the guard escorted me into the Shantel village and straight to the sakkri's hut, giving me no time to compose myself or look for Kadee. Inside, the elderly priestess was conversing with a fair-haired woman.

The falcon was wearing slim leggings, high boots, and a low-backed bodice that left bare the place where she would have worn wings on the falcon homeland, Ahnmik. She didn't seem to be armed, but a master of Ahnmik's magic didn't need to be.

"Charis?" I asked, assuming this was the falcon Nathaniel had borrowed from Jaguar.

The falcon spun about as if startled. *"Hehj?"*

Instantly, I realized every assumption I had made was wrong. The wide eyes that stared at me with apparent excitement were pale green, more like my brother's or sister's than any falcon I had ever met, and there were no traces of blue or violet power in her hair. Her skin was fair by local standards, but did not have the unnatural porcelain color it should have.

She was a falcon. I was sure of it. But I was equally sure that this girl had less power than I did.

Her expression held bright hope. "You know Charis?" she asked in the falcon's native language.

I looked toward the sakkri, hoping she could explain what was going on.

"We have struggled to communicate clearly," the sakkri

said. "Our languages have some similarities, but many differences, and she does not seem to speak the native tongue. I believe she was on her way to Midnight."

I nodded, dazed. The more powerful falcons spoke multiple languages, but this one was *ka'jaes*, without magic, which meant she had probably never been taught anything but the language of Ahnmik. *"Hehj'rsh'hena?"* I asked. *Who are you?*

I could tell from her wince that my pronunciation was off, but I was trying to speak a language I had literally learned through childhood *dreams*. She should be grateful I spoke her tongue at all.

"La ..." She responded in her own language, just as haltingly, though surely for other reasons. *"La'Keyi'nasa'ha 'o'Alain'ra'o'aona'Araceli."*

I repeated the foreign words, not because I didn't understand them, but because I didn't understand how they were *possible*. This powerless slip of a girl was claiming to be an emissary for Lord Alain, son of the heir to the falcon empress. That seemed odd enough, but in giving her name, she had included none of the lengthy titles of which falcons were so proud.

Of course she doesn't have a title, I thought. *She's ka'jaes.*

I reached toward her magically, opening myself up to the swirls of fate and prophecy that danced around every living creature.

Mistake.

She had no power, but somewhere on her person, she was wearing a talisman embedded with the magic of the royal house of Ahnmik. When my poorly disciplined power brushed over it, I was dragged into a tornado of politics, passion, intrigue, and betrayal.

"I gave Charis more freedom than her birth would have allowed her. I allowed her . . . many freedoms." Alain paused, then, finally, he confided, *"I knew what she was doing. I tried to ignore it, but once her treason became too loud, I couldn't let it go. Charis would have gotten herself killed if she had gone through with her plans, and she would have brought a lot of people down with her. And it never would have worked."*

"I was never really privy to her plans," Keyi said. *"Mostly . . . we played chess."*

"What are you doing here?" I asked, in the rhythmical language of Ahnmik. The vision wasn't clear enough for me to understand what relationship this powerless girl had to the most powerful man in Ahnmik, or the falcon who had been sold to Jaguar.

"My lord sent me to assess the strength of the vampires' empire, to advise him as to whether an alliance would be profitable." She frowned. "Something knocked me from the sky."

My stomach sank. I shuddered to imagine Mistress Jeshickah and the falcon empress, two near immortals with a thirst for power and nothing but ice in their souls, allied.

The sun itself would fall before them.

We were lucky the girl had made the mistake of travel-ing over Shantel land.

"To whom am I speaking?" the ka'jaes—*Keyi*, she had called herself—asked testily.

Truth, or lie? Most falcons could sense a lie, but this one didn't have the power to do so.

"*La'Malachi'ra'Obsidian,*" I answered, erring—unusually enough, for me—on the side of the truth.

The words clearly answered none of her questions.

"But who *are* you? Did my lord send you to check on me?" she asked nervously.

"Why would he need to check on you?"

I tried again, and this time got a clearer picture of the situation.

Two women, sitting at a chessboard.

"*They'll let this entire world die if they continue this way,*" *Charis grumbled as she moved her bishop across the board to take Keyi's rook. "Did you know it has been nearly a century since there has been a pureblood birth that did not result in a ka'jaes child?"*

Charis considered the fact that she was alive and sane despite being half crow a sign that the empress was unnecessarily destroy-ing their world through her laws against quemak *children.*

"*Pureblood* ranked *birth,*" *Keyi corrected absently as she considered her next move. "Risha was executed last week." Ka'jaes falcons conceived far more easily than magic users, but doing so was as forbidden as the conception of* quemak. *Risha* had been allowed to deliver her child–the empress would never allow the destruction of an infant, unborn or not–and then put to death.

"My apologies," Charis said. "Your kind and mine are the exceptions."

Though Keyi claimed to speak for the son of the heir to the Empress, if she had followed Charis, she was as guilty of treason as her predecessor.

Once again, I used the truth.

"I'm *quemak*," I admitted, and saw her eyes widen. "I was born in Midnight." Many of Ahnmik's words had shades of meaning. The word I used for "born" was not the one usually used for children. This one could just as easily mean "created." It was more accurate. "I have never been to Ahnmik, and I owe no loyalty to the falcon royal house." She flinched instinctively at those words, which would have been treason if I had spoken them to . . . no, they *were* treason. If this girl reported back to the royal house about my existence, Ahnmik might very well feel the need to get rid of me. They had ways of tracking a traitor that were a good deal more frightening than those the serpiente employed.

If she doesn't choose to side with us, we will have to kill her, I thought. *She has so little power, the royal house won't be able to tell exactly what happened to her.*

"You're loyal to Midnight?" she asked.

I looked at the sakkri, who had been waiting patiently,

and said, "I don't know what value she has in terms of Nathaniel's plan, but I think it's worth bringing her in as an ally." Better than having a woman with the ear of the royal house on any other side.

"I concur. She's a catalyst," the sakkri said. "Like you are."

"Catalyst?" I asked.

"Your being in a place and time changes it," she elaborated. "You walk through visions and use those visions to guide you even when you think you are blind. How else did you end up here today when we needed you?"

"Nathaniel sent me."

"You made Nathaniel send you," the sakkri said. "He does not know yet that she is here."

Keyi cleared her throat, clearly irritated that we were speaking around her in a language she didn't understand.

"I apologize," I said, switching back to the falcon tongue. "I needed to explain the situation. As for my loyalty, I am as loyal to Midnight as you are to Ahnmik." Her eyes widened, and I saw the instinct to protest, but I didn't let her continue. "Charis was your leader, wasn't she?"

I could see her weighing the risks of answering honestly, and considering the treason I had spoken myself, before she said, "Yes. Alain sent her to Midnight as punishment for her treason . . . or for getting caught, anyway. He thinks a poor, powerless peasant like myself will be too grateful for his royal attention to hold a grudge and too stupid to realize he will get rid of me the same way when I cease to be useful. Is she alive?"

The falcon royal house made Jeshickah's arrogance look like nerves. Then again, they made her power look like a child playing house, too.

"Alive, yes," I answered. "I do not know if she is well, but I think I can bring her here." Of the sakkri, I asked, "How quickly can you get a message to Nathaniel?"

"Within moments," she answered. "He is carrying a talisman of ours."

"Tell him to bring Charis here," I said. If Charis wasn't broken, she would surely tell Keyi that the last thing the world needed was a Midnight-falcon alliance. And if it was too late for Charis, that too would make the point I wanted.

While we waited for Nathaniel and Charis, I looked for Kadee. I wished Keyi would stay behind with the sakkri, but wasn't surprised that she followed the one person she had found who spoke her language.

I found Kadee practicing her archery with some of the Shantel hunters. When she saw me, she dropped her bow—causing quite a few winces from the Shantel around her—and ran to my side.

"I've been losing my mind waiting for word from you and Vance!" she snapped. "I feel like I've been put out of the way. No one tells me anything." She grabbed my hand

and pulled me toward her campsite, and out of the range of the others' hearing. Only belatedly, she seemed to notice Keyi. "Who's your friend?"

"This is Keyi. She's on our side, or will be soon," I answered. "I think Nathaniel meant to put me out of the way, too."

If he hadn't known about Keyi, the only reason he would have sent me to Shantel land was to get me out of Midnight so I wouldn't get in more trouble. I intended to have a few words with him on that subject.

Kadee looked equally determined to address the matter when the messenger arrived to tell us Nathaniel was waiting for us. Despite the current alliance, he wasn't allowed in the Shantel village, so we met him and the falcon at a clearing in the woods.

Charis's downcast eyes were the deep violet of the more powerful members of her kind, but her dark hair must have come from her crow heritage. She was *quemak*, like me, but so powerful it made my teeth ache.

Keyi's gaze lit up when she saw her once friend and mentor, and greeted her with a rapid series of questions and exclamations; Charis's impassive, emotionless response to the other falcon's warm greeting clearly hurt her.

"How is she?" I asked Nathaniel.

"Jaguar says Alain did something to her magically that

left her . . . inconsistent. All I've seen is a fine example of a trainer's work, though."

After a few excited attempts at conversation, Keyi spun to me to demand, "What is wrong with her? She is worse than a criminal released by the Mercy."

The Mercy were Ahnmik's elite police and torturers. The things they were capable of doing to a person's mind in the name of the Empress were legendary. "Midnight's *trainers* . . ." I had to stop, because I didn't have a word for "trainer." All the words that came to mind failed to encompass the evil of Jeshickah's brood. "The blood-drinkers who rule Midnight have their own version of the Mercy," I said. "Their job is to take someone like Charis, and turn her into someone perfectly obedient, without any will of her own. It is a very thorough process." *Usually*. I thought of Alasdair.

I saw the fury in Keyi's eyes, and knew there was no danger of her siding with Midnight now.

"The sakkri says you've found us a falcon ally?" Nathaniel asked me, while sizing up Keyi with obvious skepticism. He was familiar enough with their kind to recognize her limitations as easily as I had.

"She found us," I answered. I quickly explained what I knew of Keyi's background and her relationship to Alain.

"I hope Vance is having better luck with the Azteka," Nathaniel sighed. "Having her will help, but only if we can fool the others into thinking she is more powerful than she is. More importantly, if she's with us, we'll know she isn't with Jeshickah."

I examined Keyi critically. I couldn't do anything about her eyes except hope that most people wouldn't realize what those mossy green irises meant. Most shapeshifters had more variety in their coloration than the falcons did, so that wasn't entirely a fool's hope. A falcon's "blue," however, the marks of power that streaked the hair, was a well-known distinguishing mark that even a casual observer would notice was missing.

"I can't make her pass anything more than the most cursory magical inspection," I told Nathaniel, "but I can make her a bit more convincing to a more mundane observer."

Nathaniel nodded. "It will make a difference with Shevaun, and some of the others. They're primed for a fight, but don't want to start it unless they're sure we'll win."

Keyi looked at me as if she already didn't like what I was saying, even without having the words translated.

There was one question, though, which would make or break this whole plan.

I turned to Keyi and asked, "Can you lie?"

Many pureblood falcons couldn't. The god Ahnmik who supposedly gave them their powers was also the god who held vows true and judged the honesty of words. My white-viper blood seemed to have spared me from that particular curse, but many falcons found it physically painful or outright impossible to speak anything but the truth as they understood it.

Keyi didn't hesitate. She nodded, with a slight smile spreading on her face, and asked, "How do you think I convinced Alain to send me here?"

CHAPTER 19

"IT'S NOT THE SAME!" *Ashley protested. Why wouldn't the cobra stop pushing? "When I remember who I was, I remember a mother who didn't know my name. Some days she didn't even know she had a second daughter. I remember being told it wasn't ladylike to cry and it wasn't safe to even ask why—"*

No tears. She hadn't been allowed to cry then, and she wasn't allowed to cry now. Tears were not permitted in Midnight.

Her voice cracked, and Hara pulled her forward, wrapping her arms around her. "That wasn't all your life held, even if it's all the trainer lets you remember."

"You don't know," Ashley whispered.

"I remember hearing about Lorelei's illness," Hara said.

"Illness," Ashley echoed, pulling away. "Madness, more like."

"They say Midnight did it."

Ashley shook her head. No one knew why Midnight had seen fit to make an example out of her mother, Tuuli Thea Lorelei, only that they had. Her sister, Miriam, had come to the throne early, and Alasdair had faded into the background.

"You were put here by your enemies," Ashley whispered. "I was put here by my own foolishness."

Living among the Shantel felt like standing in the eye of a storm. The king and princes avoided me, though I wasn't sure if it was out of respect for my beliefs or general distaste for my existence. As royals, they would have known both Alasdair and Hara, and perhaps had been friendly with them.

I hadn't told Nathaniel that I intended to get Alasdair out during the attack because he would only tell me not to, but as often as I could, I used my power to peer into Gabriel's rooms to observe the two women there.

Nathaniel still refused to involve the avians in his plan, claiming that he couldn't trust them. Listening to Alasdair's description of her mother's decline, I understood why he thought Lorelei's people might be too frightened to risk involvement.

"It's time," Nathaniel said to me now, startling me from an attempt to scry into the serpiente palace. In addition to Alasdair and Hara, I tried to keep an eye on Misha, but her power made doing so difficult.

With a little over a month left until the equinox, Nathaniel had once again summoned our allies to Shantel land, this time without magic concealing our identities. The nighttime air was crisp, and the fog was lighter than it had been the last time I was in this clearing, but the sliver of waxing moon above seemed to create more shadows than it cleared.

The sakkri was deep in conversation with Keyi, who had used a combination of lemon juice and woad dye to lighten most of her hair and then add the blue streaks that would help her pass as a more powerful falcon. The sakkri had helped expand the aura of magic from Alain's token so it seemed to encompass the otherwise powerless falcon—an illusion that would pass most superficial magical examinations. They still sometimes struggled, but a week of practice had improved the sakkri's ability to make sense of the falcon's language.

Not far away, Theron's fledgling Shevaun was laughing at a comment Adjila had just made. *Powerful and not squeamish,* Nathaniel had called that witch. If either of them were nervous, they hid it well.

The Macht witches were both visible this time, the blond Sara who had offered Aislinn a home if she was willing to disobey Nathaniel and another witch with dark hair and blue eyes. They stood furthest back, their postures anxious but determined. Sara looked up and scowled as she caught me staring.

Who were the others? There were two more vampires

in the group, one man and one woman, both unfamiliar to me. They stood together, the woman shielding herself from the witches' view with her companion's body. Unless there was someone else we hadn't heard from yet, he had to be the representative from Silver's line who had needled Nathaniel at the previous meeting.

There was also a man I was pretty sure was a shape-shifter, who occasionally exchanged words with the others as he paced the dark forest.

The only face still hidden was the cloaked figure I had noticed last time, who had to be Nathaniel's employer. Who had been bold enough—and wealthy enough—to hire Nathaniel for such an incredible mission?

When Nathaniel stepped into the clearing, all eyes turned toward him. He looked around the crowd, took a breath, and greeted each individual by name.

"Sakkri of the Shantel. Shevaun, daughter of Kendra, and Adjila, student of Pandora. Sara Vida, and Averill Arun—"

Averill protested, "There is no need—"

"There is absolute need," Nathaniel argued. "I allowed you to maintain your anonymity last time because some of you were unwilling to commit to our cause until you knew we could win. It is now too late to back out . . . and any one of us who is discovered after today is likely to be hunted down and visited with a most grisly demise. Since I wear *my* name openly, it seems only right that you do as well."

"Get on with it," Sara sighed. "I don't want to be here longer than I need to."

Nathaniel continued.

"Kral, of the Mistari and the Bruja guilds," he greeted the pacing shapeshifter, "and Malachi Obsidian." When he said my name, I felt a pulse of power. Nathaniel wasn't just introducing us; he was binding us in some kind of spell. At this point, I had no option but to hope it was a spell for our benefit. He greeted the other vampires as "Jager, of Silver's line, and the good lady Lila, of Macht and Kendra's lines." The two witches, Averill and Sara, both tensed and exchanged sharp whispers. A witch turned vampire—no wonder they were so disturbed by her. Nathaniel turned to Keyi to say, "And finally, *shm'Ahnmik'la'Keyi'jaes'oisna'o na'saniet.*"

Indigo Choir and Empress's Mercy; quite a title to falsely claim for our powerless friend. The sakkri, aware of our ruse, was silent at the lie.

"And who is *that*?" Averill's voice rang out across the clearing as she pointed toward the hooded figure.

"Witch," Shevaun snapped, "I am in the mood to bloody my hands tonight. Shut your mouth and stop delaying this infernal meeting if you do not want that blood to be yours."

"Thank you, Shevaun," Nathaniel sighed. He looked toward the sakkri. "Are we still expecting one more?"

"Any moment," the sakkri answered. "I have stretched

time and space to make this circle secure. Her magic resisted, so her travel was somewhat delayed."

That sounded promising. "Azteka?" I asked Nathaniel. "Is Vance back?" He knew Kadee and I had been anxiously awaiting Vance's return.

Nathaniel gave me an enigmatic smile, but refused to confirm my guess. I bit my tongue only because now was not the time to shake the information from him.

"You know how much I hate being bored," Shevaun called. "Can we get on with this?"

Nathaniel's calm expression never broke, but I could sense his nervousness as he said, "We should be—" He straightened, and I followed his gaze through the trees, where a feline too dense to be one of the lithe cougars and leopards of the Shantel had just come into view. The jaguar was followed by a small bird whose long green tail trailed after him like a pennant—Vance.

Seeing him safely returned, I let go of tension I hadn't even realized I was holding in my shoulders. I reached a hand into my pocket and grasped a carved sigil, thinking, *Vance is back. He's safe.* Thanks to the magic of Shantel witches who were fond of and anxious to take care of our half-serpent friend, the thought would find its way to Kadee. Nathaniel wanted to limit the number of people directly involved in his plan, and refused to accept a fifteen-year-old half serpent as one of his fighters, but I wasn't willing to keep her ignorant of our plans.

The jaguar with Vance returned to human form. Her body was lean and powerful, and the russet skin on her arms was decorated with the ritualistic scars of a powerful bloodwitch. I recognized her immediately. The last time I had seen her, she had just executed the Shantel witch who had nearly killed the trainers. The act saved my life, along with Vance's and Kadee's, but if she had only stayed her hand another day, who knew what would have happened?

"Vance Ehecatl of the Obsidian guild, and Lady Alejandra, priestess of Malinalxochitl," Nathaniel said formally, binding them both into the spell with us. Vance came to my side as Alejandra stayed to speak with Nathaniel. "You are with us?"

"I am," Alejandra replied. "The priesthood and royal class still insist Midnight is not a significant threat to our nation, and they do not want to risk a true bloodwitch falling into the vampires' hands, but I am able to act alone because I can claim kinship."

"Kinship?" I asked Vance, struggling to keep my voice from revealing my selfish dismay. If Vance had discovered blood relatives among the Azteka, would he still want to stay with Obsidian?

Vance shook his head.

"If he survives the assault," Alejandra continued, still speaking to Nathaniel as if the rest of us were not present, "I claim the right to take custody of Jaguar de Fiaro. We share parentage."

Nathaniel's brows raised, and I could tell he was trying to suppress laughter as he answered, "If he survives, I'll see that none of our people fights you for him." *Who would want to?* I could see him thinking.

"Share . . . he's your *brother?*" I asked, after replaying her words through my mind twice. "How is that even possible?" Everyone knew Jaguar had Azteka heritage, but he was also hundreds of years old. Would Vance live that long? And if Jaguar's sister was a bloodwitch, shouldn't he have been, too?

Alejandra looked past me to speak to Vance, clearly more concerned that another born bloodwitch might be more upset than she was about a half falcon's curiosity. "Our magic can be used to extend life by many years. Untrained, you will have a more normal life span."

"Jaguar is half human," Vance replied. "Or, was."

Alejandra nodded slightly. "As am I. It is why I am not able to pass my magic down to my children—though it does *not* in any way limit my own power," she added, turning her attention to the group around us for the first time. "I regret I've been so hesitant to address the problem of Midnight before now, even though it took my own blood relative from me long ago. I am honored to stand with you all now."

The two Macht witches nodded as if they admired and agreed with Alejandra's proud sentiments. Shevaun snickered. I was beginning to like the irreverent vampire, though I suspected she wouldn't hesitate to kill me if the whim came to her. I wished I were bold enough to laugh at what I knew we would soon face.

"*Now* we are ready," the sakkri said. "Nathaniel, tell us your plan."

I already knew some of Nathaniel's plan, and could guess which of our allies would object to it. Adjila would be fine, and Shevaun and the other vampires wouldn't hesitate, but the Macht witches wouldn't want to sacrifice their once-kin. The Shantel already executed escaped slaves on sight, believing they couldn't be trusted; the sakkri probably already knew what Nathaniel would say. I wasn't sure about Kral, Alejandra, or Keyi.

Nathaniel bowed his head, and spoke softly, not looking toward any of us.

"Midnight has allies in every major civilization—yes, including the witches who say they exist purely to fight Midnight," Nathaniel said, with a pointed look to Sara and Averill. "If we want to strike Midnight through the vampires, we would be looking at killing over a dozen of them, at *least,* in order to ensure Midnight does not rebuild. In the process, we would need to cross creatures with enough power to wipe any of us entirely off the map, who would avenge those deaths in a mass slaughter that would make Midnight's reign look like Eden."

"After weeks of planning, you tell us it *can't be done?*" Sara demanded, clearly outraged.

"No," Nathaniel snapped. "These weeks of planning have made it clear how it *must* be done. We cannot destroy the vampires, but we *can* destroy their empire, thoroughly enough that Silver's line can step forward and eliminate any opportunity for Midnight to rebuild."

"You mean to destroy the property instead of the owners," Kral said. "Will that work?"

"It will work as long as someone else steps in to control Jeshickah and her kin while they are weak," Jager answered. "We'll make sure that happens."

Predictably, Sara was the one who raised her voice to object. "When you say 'property' you don't just mean buildings. You're talking about slaves. You're talking about killing hundreds of people, some our own flesh and blood."

"They *used to be*," Nathaniel echoed. "Now they're not."

"We saw that demonstration," Averill said quietly. "Any of our kin would be willing to give their lives if it means ending this empire. But what happens after that? Is this new leadership any better?"

All eyes turned to Jager, my own included. Would he assure us all that his line would be wise and generous leaders?

Instead, he laughed. "There is absolutely nothing I can say to you that you will trust. So what's the point?" Lila whispered something to him, and he sighed. "Fine. If it helps, I'll tell you this. I've been a slave. I don't approve. One of my line was once a shapeshifter. She says we should let them be. One of us used to be a witch. She . . . honestly, she doesn't care what we do with you, but we have no reason to exterminate you and no desire to subjugate you. And though my friend here is not of my line," he added, looking at Lila, "I value her highly, and she speaks quite fiercely on your behalf. Does that help?"

Averill and Sara exchanged a heavy look, and dropped their objections. I considered pressing for more information, but what else was there to ask? If he was being honest, we would all be much better off after Silver's line took over. If he was lying, there was no way for me to force the truth from him.

"Even if Silver's line says they can help control their kind afterward," Sara argued reasonably, "surely it would be more direct to just cut the head off the snake—*Mistress* Jeshickah."

Nathaniel exchanged a look with the robed figure, who nodded. "Jeshickah keeps the hunters who have tried that as her personal pets," Nathaniel said. "You may yet encounter some when they fight to protect their mistress. Protecting us from their magic is part of what I need you for in this fight. And if you did succeed," he continued, "you would shortly thereafter find yourself experiencing pain beyond the scope of your imagination, at the hands either of Jeshickah's kin, or the true immortals who protect her.

Silver's line might not want to exterminate your kind, but if you cross Jeshickah's allies, they will destroy every last man, woman, and child of your bloodline. Starting with your daughter . . . Elisabeth, right?"

Sara reached over her shoulder for a knife, and suddenly the forest was a sea of weapons. I stepped back into the deeper shadows of the forest, hoping my power would keep me and Vance unnoticed if this meeting turned bloody. The only people who did not draw steel—aside from myself— were Jager, Alejandra, the sakkri, and Keyi. Keyi didn't know how to fight. The others' expressions said clearly that they needed no weapons to defend themselves.

Before Sara's blade had even cleared its sheath, Shevaun was on her, deflecting her arm. Averill moved to defend her fellow witch; all Adjila did was reach out and touch her arm, but I heard Averill scream.

Chaos. I stopped trying to track what was going on. Had Nathaniel anticipated this? Did he have a plan to stop it? I looked up and caught his gaze an instant before Keyi stepped forward, shouting, *"Enough!"*

Her voice rang through the forest, sending a pulse of power through the web Nathaniel had wrapped us all in. The sakkri's magic caused her voice to echo in a more familiar language.

All around me, I saw combatants hesitate.

"One doesn't need to be native to this land to understand we are mostly enemies, or at the best, neutral toward each other," Keyi said. "That gives us plenty of room to bicker like children, as doubtless you have done since Midnight first rose, as doubtless you have done over the years as Midnight enslaved your loved ones. I have been told that Midnight encourages such conflict to ensure none can successfully stand against them. We can continue to fight now if you wish—or we can stop stalling and cast our lots. Ahnmik declares that *Midnight must fall.* Are we in agreement?"

There was silence for long moments as the others reacted, some gratefully and some resentfully.

Alejandra spoke first. "I speak for the followers of Malinalxochitl and the Azteka: Midnight must fall."

Next was Kral. "I and mine are with you."

Sara and Averill exchanged glances, and finally Sara said, "I would rather a more . . . direct solution, but anything that will weaken Jeshickah's empire must be done. We are with you."

Nathaniel took over, and addressed each of the rest in turn.

"Shevaun?"

The vampiress grinned. "As ever, willing to fight."

"Adjila?"

The witch wrapped an arm around Shevaun's waist. "As my lady wishes."

"Obsidian?"

I shivered when he looked at me, fighting to suppress

the echoes and competing voices of all the possible futures, all waiting for our decision. I swallowed hard, and could only nod wordlessly.

"Lila?"

I saw the two witches tense again as the golden-haired vampire nodded. "I am with you." Lila looked to Sara and Averill, and added sadly, "With my once-sisters."

"Does this suit you?" Nathaniel asked of Jager, who nodded. Turning to the hooded figure, he added, "And you?" The cloaked figure also nodded, though the movement was hesitant. Apparently I wasn't the only one wondering where this mob might go.

"And the Shantel?"

All eyes turned to the sakkri.

"We are with you."

"You all know your assignments. I brought us together today to make sure we are all clear on our intentions, and to get any . . . unpleasant surprises out of the way. We have only five weeks left before the fall equinox, and much to do in that time. Any questions?" Nathaniel asked. He let several seconds pass in silence before saying, "Good. I will see you all back here at sunset, September the twenty-second."

And on that night, if the ever-fickle Fate was on our side, we would destroy the world as we knew it.

CHAPTER 20

"I'M RUNNING OUT OF TIME," *Lorelei hissed in a savage whisper that chilled Alasdair to the bone. "I tried, my daughter. I tried so hard. When you are queen, you will understand."*

Alasdair bit her lip, knowing it was useless to argue. It wasn't the first time since this illness had come on that Lorelei had mistaken her for Miriam. Usually, she spoke as if Alasdair were still seven, instead of almost twenty. Occasionally, Lorelei forgot she had a second daughter at all.

"Yes, Mother," Alasdair agreed, because the blazing golden eyes staring at her would allow nothing else.

"That . . . that's good," Lorelei said, nodding. Her grip relaxed, and Alasdair was able to pull away. "Run along, then. You're late to your lessons."

Alasdair left as slowly and politely as she could stand to, but it was still too quickly to be seemly. Fleeing that sickroom and returning to her own room wasn't sufficient. Her heart was hammering in her chest and she knew if she didn't get away, she would start screaming and never stop. Then the avian court would have two mad royal women instead of one.

She took to the sky. She had no destination, but every time she considered turning around the panic returned, so she kept flying. Eventually, hours past sundown, she ran out of solid earth and landed in a small port town that stank of salt water, ships' cargo, and human sweat.

She changed into human form in an empty alleyway. As soon as she stepped onto the street, she knew she was out of place, and in danger. Too many eyes fell on her, and most of them weren't friendly . . . or were too friendly, in a predatory way she couldn't help but understand. When she tried to return to her hawk form, though, her vision swirled. She was too exhausted to flee.

"You look lost, beautiful."

She turned toward the new voice, which was kind and soothing and belonged to a man whose dark eyes were simultaneously gentle and intense. The brutes on the street, many of whom had moved toward her when she appeared in their midst, saw who had come to champion her and suddenly found other things to do.

"Anything?" Alejandra asked as I pulled out of the vision with a gasp.

I shook my head. I had tried to see the attack on Midnight, to help us anticipate otherwise unforeseen dangers, but my ever-unreliable power had found an image from the past instead. Alasdair's words to Hara—*You were put here by your enemies. I was put here by my own foolishness*—had needled me since I first heard them.

I didn't want to know why she felt responsible. No one deserved what she had gone through. But the visions that might let me help ourselves and therefore help *her* refused to come.

"Sorry," I said.

Alejandra nodded, undaunted by my failure. This wasn't the first time I had attempted to spy into our future in the two weeks since we had started working together, and most of my efforts had been equally unhelpful. Alejandra had been equally nonplussed when the sakkri had explained that her visions did not come at will, and only showed futures that were inevitable; the upcoming weeks were still too uncertain for her to see them clearly.

"I'm starting to agree with Kadee about how irritating prophecy is, anyway," Vance remarked, his gaze straying to where the young serpent was once again working with the Shantel hunters. It was clear that Vance wished he could join that group, but he had been lumped in with us magic users for planning the attack on Midnight.

"I have nearly completed the spell for the slaves," Alejandra said, moving on in her ever-practical way. "It will cause the madness and violence Nathaniel wishes, but in order to use it precisely, it needs to be contained in a conscious vessel. Someone needs to carry the spell in their veins, to control how it is passed on, and to whom, and to trigger the final phase at the time of the attack."

Her gaze had barely flickered to Vance before he said, "No."

I opened my mouth to ask how dangerous the task would be, but Alejandra cut me off. "Surely you will not attempt to coerce a born bloodwitch whose blood has already once been used to incubate a poison without his consent?"

I didn't need Alejandra to warn me from pressing the issue; it would never have occurred to me to put Vance in that position. Whoever triggered the riot was likely to die in it, either at the hands of the trainers who came to subdue the fighting or at the flames that would then devour the building.

"Could someone else carry the spell?" I asked. "I'm not a bloodwitch, but I have some power, and I have as much access to Midnight as Vance would." And it would give me a reason to be inside so I could go for Alasdair.

"I'm . . . not sure if you could serve," Alejandra answered. "Come here."

When I obeyed, she held out a hand. I sighed before offering her my own, which she turned palm up. She drew a small obsidian blade, uttered an invocation under her breath, and then pierced the skin of my wrist just enough for a single drop of blood to bead on the surface.

Alejandra touched the blood, closed her eyes as she rubbed it between her fingertips, and then grimaced. She recoiled from me, and wiped her hand on a rag.

"No," she said, swallowing thickly.

"What's wrong with him?" Vance asked, concerned by Alejandra's disgusted reaction.

She shook her head. "His power is . . ." She shuddered. "It isn't compatible with ours. That is all."

I wondered what it was that offended her. The madness of the falcons? Something about my white-viper heritage?

"Do you need a bloodwitch for this?" Vance asked reluctantly. Last time, it had been a Shantel poison he had brought into Midnight. Vance hadn't known about the spell until it had already almost succeeded. I could imagine how he would feel now, being asked once more to act as a vessel for such power.

"I may be able to place the power inside a human," Alejandra said, "as long as he or she is otherwise untouched by magic."

"We won't send you in there," I assured Vance.

"I'll go if it's our only option," he offered, his voice small.

"We will make sure it is not our only option," Alejandra said.

May I have some of your time?

I jumped as the sakkri's voice floated through my head.

It wasn't the first time she had done that, but it never got less unsettling. I excused myself from Vance and Alejandra, and walked to the sakkri's tent.

The first thing I noticed once inside was an iron bowl full of a viscous fluid that pulsed as if alive. The hypnotic, glimmering light that emanated from it made my eyes water and fill with spots as if I were looking straight into the sun, and yet it took incredible effort to look away. When I did, cold sweat broke out on my brow.

"What is *that*?" I gasped.

"A distillation of heat and power," she answered. "Shantel, Azteka, shm'Ahnmik, Macht. It needs to cure longer, but then we will hammer it into the weapons for the attack. Anything it hits will burn."

I looked back to the cauldron of deadly magic and, even though it was exactly what we needed, I shuddered at the feel of it. "How did you get falcon power?"

"Lord Alain gave Keyi a talisman containing his blood and magic in order to mark her as his," the sakkri answered. "We were able to tie the spell to the royal falcon line through that. But you are not needed for the fire spell. You have another use."

I was strangely relieved. Maybe it was just falcon prejudice against mixing blood, but it felt *wrong*.

"What can I do for you?"

"Within these woods, I could conceal an entire world

from the vampires, but once we leave here, I am weaker," the sakkri said. "The riot will distract the vampires for a few minutes, but if we want to survive after that, we need to be well hidden. My efforts to create a spell that will work outside this forest have failed so far, so I am hoping your guild's reputation for such power is not exaggerated."

I had often helped hide my kin from angry serpiente guards, but it would be far harder to hide a force that was actively attacking.

"I'll do anything I can, but it won't hold long."

"If we work together, hopefully we can extend both our powers."

By the time the sakkri and I parted, it was well past sunset.

Kadee had already built up the campfire at the edge of Shantel land. When I went to find him, Vance was struggling to keep his eyes politely focused as Alejandra explained that there might be times when she could use his power to support her own if he let her. "But only if you feel comfortable with that. A bloodwitch must never draw his own blood, or let it be drawn, except with deliberate and holy purpose in mind."

I think she lost him on the word "holy." Vance knew his blood was too powerful to throw about carelessly, but he had no interest in the religious dogma that went with Alejandra's magic. He responded eagerly when I quoted one of Alejandra's maxims—*You must maintain your body in order to respect your power*—in order to free him to join us for dinner.

"Three weeks left," Kadee sighed. "What did the sakkri want today?"

"Help with the illusion spells that will keep us all from getting killed," I answered, rubbing my temples. My power wasn't as repulsive to the sakkri as it was to Alejandra, but it was still difficult to mesh white viper and Shantel magics. Hopefully the next three weeks would be enough for us to find a balance and come up with something useful. "How was hunting?"

"Tracking, today," Kadee answered idly. "I also learned a new way to prepare elk thistle." Nathaniel wouldn't let Kadee be directly involved in the attack on Midnight, but she was still able to help the Shantel stockpile supplies to distribute to the other shapeshifters after Midnight fell. "How are the serpiente doing?"

"Misha has guards patrolling the forest to detain anyone trying to flee to Midnight." My magic refused to let me see the future, but I had been able to sneak peeks of the present, both in serpiente land and in Midnight.

I knew Gabriel remained restless and distracted, his absences from Midnight growing longer and more frequent; Ashley was terrified that he had lost interest, and would give in to Jaguar's requests to buy her. Hara was alive and uncollared. Gabriel hadn't completely ignored

240

her, but seemed content to occasionally amuse himself with the cobra instead of focusing his attention on breaking her.

Vance fell back on his sleeping mat with a sigh. "Alejandra is going to ask Nathaniel if Aislinn can be trusted to carry the cuatlapololiztli spell." At Kadee's blank look, he said, "I think she is determined to teach me her language along with everything else. That's what she calls the spell to make all the slaves start fighting the trainers."

"Only the slaves in the north and east wings," I said. "She won't be able to get to the personal slaves." I almost stopped there, but if I couldn't trust these two, who could I trust? "And that's for the best. I plan to get Alasdair out during the attack."

Vance looked like he wanted to object, but Kadee spoke first, saying, "Good. That will give you an opportunity to get Hara out, too."

I opened my mouth to say that probably wasn't a good idea. Hara might not be completely broken, but did we will really want a traumatized, half-mad cobra out in the world? One look at Kadee, though, made it clear this question wasn't up for debate. If I refused to save Hara—or at least try—Kadee would never forgive me.

In the end, I valued our family more than I valued my fear or dislike of the serpiente royal house.

"The others are going to let you do that?" Vance asked.

"I wasn't planning to ask permission. Once I'm done

helping the sakkri set the illusion spells, it won't matter if I slip away."

"You won't be able to go through the front gate," Vance pointed out, fiddling with a bandage on his arm. His blood and Alejandra's had both gone into the spell. "Within minutes of the start of the attack, the fire there will be impassable."

"There is a back door," I explained. "It's used to bring in large shipments of supplies or to haul out corpses. I think Nathaniel is planning to use it to enable Aislinn to escape after she starts the riot in the south wing." Nathaniel hadn't actually shared that detail with anyone, probably for the same reason I hadn't told anyone I planned to rescue Gabriel's beloved "Ashley." This plan rested on our allies believing us that any slave rescued from Midnight would be a paving stone that would help the trainers rebuild. We couldn't make that argument, then turn around and explain exceptions. But I could tell he cared more about Aislinn than he let on.

"Isn't that the door that Kral is going to be guarding?" Kadee asked. That particular shapeshifter was, thankfully, not staying with the Shantel. He apparently fell into the group Nathaniel considered too bloodthirsty to safely reside with the rest of us for weeks. "Will he let you by?"

I shrugged. "I'm sure he won't *let* me, but I'll get by."

I doubted Kral would hesitate to shoot me if he saw me coming out that door, but that was the crux of the issue: *if he saw me.* I would be concealed by a combination of my own magic and the sakkri's. If I could avoid the fire, I thought I could slip into Midnight and back out past Kral without his even noticing I was there.

"Do you need backup?" Kadee asked.

"Absolutely *not*," I replied vehemently. "I need you somewhere safe." She bristled, about to protest that she could handle herself, so I continued quickly. "I know you can hold your own in a fight. I know you're quick on your feet and you're clever. But you don't have wings, and if I need to escape fast, I'll probably go by air."

"Hara won't be able to—"

I cut her off. "I won't die for Hara," I said flatly. "I would give my life before I ran and left *you* to burn, or Vance, but I won't make the same sacrifice for a cobra."

I waited for her to fight me, but instead, her argumentative expression dissolved, replaced by something more sentimental. A child of Obsidian generally looked out for himself first, and others second. But I meant what I had said: I had lost too many already. I wouldn't lose Vance or Kadee, not if I could help it.

Vance reached over and squeezed my hand.

For a minute, we all sat in silence. Finally, Kadee asked me, "You still can't see anything about our future?"

"No," I said. "I just end up looking at the past instead."

If we couldn't completely crush Midnight, their

retaliation would be swift and horrific. And if we did win, what next? The target of Misha's wrath would be gone, and I didn't know how that would affect her. Empowered by prophecy and success, would she get stronger, perhaps even becoming a queen to be proud of? Or would she unravel as her last purpose was taken from her?

When it was time for sleep, I stretched my bedroll out not far from the fire. Kadee and Vance lay close enough that I could have rolled over and touched either one of them. I could feel Vance's warmth barely inches from my back, and when I closed my eyes, I could hear his rapid heartbeat.

At least for now, as we all faced an uncertain future, we rested like serpiente, comforting each other with our nearness.

CHAPTER 21

"I WOULD LIKE *to see you again."*

Alasdair hesitated. She hated pulling out of his arms, but she knew perfectly well that she should never have been there in the first place.

If she had ever met a man like Gabriel before, she hadn't known it. She was an avian lady, the younger daughter of the queen. Even the serpiente she had met had always been respectfully restrained, though she had been told that among their own kind they were bold, proud, and prone to emotional displays.

Gabriel had been polite and courteous, but never hesitant or shy. He had offered to be her protector when she was still too exhausted to take her hawk's form and fly home. They had dinner, then went dancing in a small hall with none of the grace and beauty of her home but all of the rowdy energy she had never known humans possessed. By the time she had the physical strength to leave, it was the last thing she wanted to do.

"I don't think that's possible," she said, unable to keep the regret from her voice. She had responsibilities at home, not to mention suitors who were better matched to her station.

This had been a diversion—a scandalous one at that. It could never be more.

Red sky at night, sailors' delight, I thought as the sun sank on the evening of the fall equinox.

I was pretty sure this was another piece of drivel I had picked up from Misha, and so from her trainer, but I couldn't get it out of my head as I watched the orange and crimson streaks stretch across the sky through the treetops.

As the day of the attack drew near, I had finally been able to see some of what would happen tonight, but only in incoherent flashes of fire. That was how I knew the sky right then was the exact color human flesh would burn when touched by our magic.

I couldn't decide if I preferred the visions of charring flesh or the occasional glimpses of Alasdair's early infatuation with the man who would later enslave her. She had thought Gabriel human, and assumed he had no idea who she was. I was sure he had recognized her the moment she stepped out of the alley.

Now, in the Shantel forest, Nathaniel had gathered his allies one last time before the attack. Kadee and Vance had both been sent back to the Shantel village; they wouldn't be involved in the final, dangerous slaughter.

Looking around, I counted thirteen of us, including the mercenary who had brought us all together.

Nathaniel drew a deep breath, and reviewed our plan one last time.

"Shevaun, Adjila. You two are on the properties outside Midnight proper: the greenhouse, the di'Birgetta estate, Taro's and Varick's homes, Gabriel's home in Dockside and Jeshickah's estate—watch yourself, there's at least one witch guarding that last one." He looked to me, and added, "Stay clear of the village and the farms. We're leaving them for the shapeshifters to scavenge."

They each nodded, even Shevaun holding her normally acerbic tongue.

"The sakkri and Malachi are responsible for the illusion spell that will keep the rest of us from being noticed. Keyi and Alejandra will be with them by the front entrance to sustain the fire spell. Lila and Jager, you're to their right side; Sara and Averill, you're to their left. Kral, you're on the back entrance with me. Cut down anyone who attempts to flee the building, and keep the trainers busy when they come out to fight. We need to keep them off the magic users as long as possible."

"If the trainers engage us," Sara asked, "can we defend ourselves?"

"Once I have Jaguar in my line of sight, I can control

him," Alejandra answered. "He at least will not be a threat to you."

"I'm more concerned about Jeshickah," Sara remarked. "If it's her or me, I'll kill her."

With a glance to our employer, Nathaniel replied, "It won't be her or you. It will be you or your entire line. I can't make that decision for you, but I know you've been working on spells that will incapacitate a vampire instead of killing. I advise you use them.

"Are we ready?" Nathaniel asked.

Silence reigned for what felt like eternity, and then the sakkri spoke once more.

"The black knight moves into check," she said, her gaze resting on Nathaniel. "The crimson queen screams. His heart rests inside the ash, smoke, and fire, rising to the sky on angel wings."

I saw Nathaniel's frame go tense as piano wire, and saw the muscles in his jaw tighten as he fought down what could only be questions.

The sakkri addressed each of us in turn, speaking her prophecy as she walked the circle.

To Shevaun and Adjila, she said, "Your path is wrought with blood, future and past. A human woman, a screaming child. The silent heart beats again."

Next she turned to Kral. "Never your dream to rise. Though spells keep you young for centuries, never your home to see again. An empire to build, power is slick as

248

raindrops, sliding . . . see your eyes in a woman's face. She is your weakness, and ever will be."

Kral scoffed audibly, but the sakkri did not seem to care as she turned to Alejandra.

"Seek him," she whispered. "Born of the same mother whatever blood runs through each now; seek him. And then beware, for the path you walk leads to darkness, until your death at a loving hand."

When she spoke to Keyi, she did so in the falcon's native language, flawlessly, as if her prophecy knew the tongue the sakkri herself did not. "Eight times eight moves to make, spaces to stand, but yours is a path of blood and in the end the white pawn falls from the board. Catalyst. Illusion is your art as you play the game ruled by the white lady. The rules bend."

When she came to me, she rested a hand on my wrist and said, "She returns, the golden queen. An instant to live, an instant to die, paths of threads, twisted around in your own magic so I cannot read them. I am sorry."

I rocked back from the prophecy. *Alasdair*. Who else could "the golden queen" mean? But the prophecy told me nothing new. I already knew I would get Alasdair out, no matter what it took.

Focused on my own thoughts, I lost track of the sakkri's words until she spoke to Jager. Though my thoughts were reeling, I struggled to listen because I sensed that he represented the future we had just chosen. "Yours is the empire that will rise," the sakkri said. "In chaos. In . . . *mayhem*. In freedom. Rule carefully. Recall this evening. No one will save you, if the world seeks to burn your realm."

She turned to stare into the fire as she raised her voice and said to all of us, "Some of you do not believe in prophecy, so my words are meaningless to you. Some of you will heed my words. Either way, the future is written. Now, Nathaniel, our black knight who leads us to destroy the tyrant . . . *now* we are ready."

Nathaniel still looked shaken by the sakkri's words. Clearly, his human slave meant more to him than he had expected when he bought her. It took him a moment to rally, and his voice was soft when he said, "Then it begins. Everyone move to your places."

I had already said goodbye to Vance and Kadee. Kadee would be working at an encampment just inside Shantel territory, tending our wounded if they came in need of aid. I wondered how many of us were likely to be just injured without being killed outright, but I was glad to know I had a healer on my side if I needed her. I was even gladder to know that, if I survived tonight, I would have someone to go home to. Vance's role in Nathaniel's plan was over now—his magic wasn't active enough to be of use in the attack, and his accuracy with a bow still left much to be desired—so he too remained behind to help Kadee and the others in any way he could.

Lucas, the Shantel's ruling prince, joined our group of

magic users, bringing the supplies we had previously prepared, and wishing us all good luck. Keyi, Alejandra, the sakkri, Lucas, and I walked in contemplative silence to the edge of Shantel land.

When the forest began to thin around us, the sakkri hesitated.

"You don't have to do this," Lucas said. His jaw was set in a hard line. I had not been privy to the arguments they must have had about this course of action, but I could imagine that they had been explosive. For as long as anyone could remember, the Shantel spirit-witch had never left her ancestral land. The only exception had been recently, when the younger sakkri had sacrificed herself to Midnight.

"Yes, I do," the sakkri replied. "You should turn back now. The time approaches quickly, and our people will need you."

"Lucas . . ." I couldn't figure out how to put my thoughts into words. *Thank you for sheltering all of us. Thank you for being prince of the first nation brave enough to stand against Midnight. I'm sorry for taking away your sakkri–again.* "Take care of Kadee and Vance."

He nodded.

The rest of us continued into Midnight's woods under cover of deepening darkness. We didn't dare take the road, for fear that one of Midnight's guards would notice our movements. The moon was two days past full, but it wouldn't have given enough light if we hadn't been familiar with navigating through undergrowth with little to guide us but our instincts and powers. Keyi traveled just behind my left shoulder, following the path I set, but the sakkri and Alejandra needed no assistance.

We reached the forest edge, within sight of Midnight proper, a few hours before the established hour of the attack.

"My sister foresaw this," the sakkri said. "I rejected her vision at first, because every law of our magic forbids violence or the shedding of blood, but now I know what she saw before she forced Lucas to sell her to the vampires. The path where we sold Shane to Midnight is dark and oppressive as far into the future as I can see."

"And the path where your sister forced us to sell *her*?" I asked, almost dreading the answer.

"That is the path we walk," the sakkri answered, staring into the distance. "On this path, the Shantel allow their sacred sakkri to leave their forest and bloody her hands in battle. Thirteen archers rain fire down on an empire. I have already shared with you and the others everything I have been able to see. Beyond that, there is simply darkness. A future either veiled from me, or else unwritten." She shuddered, her eyes focusing again as she pulled away from her power. "It is time. We must begin."

Without further conversation, we went to work.

I normally used naturally occurring formations to focus

my power, twining my spells into circles created by groves of trees or spills of boulders. Midnight didn't have any such natural circle where we needed it, so we had to create our own. Numerous Shantel witches had helped craft, carve, and summon the fetishes we now placed around our would-be circle. As I held each, I could recall the one who had made it, and what its purpose was.

Some of the glyphs, statues, and symbols were designed to help conceal us. Some would seek to minimize wounds to our people. Others would make our vision keener, and our attacks more deadly. Over the course of two hours, we created five circles arranged in a ring around Midnight proper, casting them with our power and imbuing them with the ability to hide our people from sight for as long as possible.

One by one, the other archers joined us, except for the few—Adjila and Shevaun—whose tasks lay elsewhere. They would burn even Nathaniel's home to the ground this night, though that was a matter of deflecting suspicion from him. His personal possessions and servants had already been moved to safe locations.

I could sense the magic wavering when it was nearly time.

I lifted my bow, and felt the crackle of power like static electricity imbued into the wood, the string, and most of all, into the arrow tips. Whatever they struck would catch fire, and the flames that resulted would devour anything they could reach, down to the very soil on which Midnight sat.

I waited, feeling the power of three different nations—falcon, Azteka, and Shantel—*thrumming* in the bow and using it to focus and calm myself. My work was mostly done. I had been needed to establish the circles so far from Shantel land, but the sakkri could maintain these illusions better than I, and if my shooting ended up being the difference between winning or losing today, it was already too late for us. I would stay long enough to make sure the fire at the front gates caught and no one would escape through those doors, but then I intended to go over the building by air to sneak in the back.

Now.

The signal seemed to whisper on the wind. Inside, if Aislinn and Alejandra had done their jobs right, the trainers and guards would be occupied subduing an inexplicable riot. We all hoped it would take them several minutes to realize what was going on outside.

My arrow wasn't the first, but it was one of the first to strike the ornate wooden door, spearing a carving of one of Jeshickah's favorite hunting cats—a leopard.

Flames had barely begun to leap up when I drew another arrow. I was about to release it when I saw one of the shapeshifter guards—a crow—rise into the air, opening its beak to issue a warning. My arrow speared the black bird's breast, and it fell onto the stone roof of the building, acting as tinder as magic turned its blood and sinew to fire.

The entire front entrance was soon ablaze, as well as several spots on the roof and nearby walls. I had already decided the third arrow would be my last when the door burst open and a figure stumbled out, wreathed in flames.

I recognized him. He was one of Midnight's more despicable guards, fond of throwing his weight around, using his fists, and exerting the power the vampires had given him as fully as he could. I grinned as I nocked an arrow and aimed at him, but then I saw what he was holding.

In the guard's arms was one of the smaller children from the nursery, a boy too young to walk on his own. My aim wavered. He knew. The bastard guard knew that any group that had assembled to fight Midnight probably wouldn't include cold-blooded child-killers.

No arrows flew as the guard started stumbling, coughing, toward us. He stopped to beat furiously at a flame that had caught on his arms as he rushed through the burning doorway, but the fire only spread to his sleeve. Even if we had wanted to, none of us had the power to extinguish that devouring magic.

An arrow from my left speared the guard through the knee, sending him shrieking to the ground. The boy tumbled out of his arms, and sat where he landed, dazed. He was old enough to know not to move without permission, which meant he was too close to the guard. The fire would spread to him.

I aimed my arrow at the boy, knowing that it would be a more merciful end than the flames, but at first my hand shook too hard to ensure an accurate shot.

We had all agreed that slaves couldn't be saved, that killing them would be a mercy, as well as the only way to ensure Midnight's true destruction. But then my eyes picked up the traces of tears on his ash-stained cheeks.

No tears.

That was one of the first lessons a slave in Midnight ever learned. I had picked it up mostly from the shadows of other children who had lived in the cell before me, instead of needing to have it beaten into me time and again until that basic human instinct had been overcome. Even when I learned that my siblings had been sold to Midnight, or when I watched through Alasdair's eyes as Shkei died, my sobs had been dry.

I saw the tears on this boy's face, and all that I could think was, *It's not too late for him.*

I didn't *decide*. I didn't even realize I had dropped my bow and was running until I was at the boy's side. If anyone saw where I came from, I just gave away our position, but I couldn't just watch this boy burn as he cried.

I pulled the child into my arms. His tears, silent salt trails, dripped onto my shoulder as I tried to decide what I could do with him. Where—

I spun toward a noise from behind me, to find Gabriel Donovan a few feet away. His dark eyes narrowed as he surveyed the area, trying to locate the source of the attack. I couldn't defend myself with the boy in my arms; I could only hope the trainer would assume I was on his side, not an enemy.

An arrow hissed toward him, but he dodged before it could strike full-on. The arrowhead cut a thin strip across his arm, but the impact wasn't direct enough to trigger the fire, which only ignited when the arrow hit the foliage beyond. The failed shot was enough for the vampire to locate the source of the attack, though. I heard a scuffle as he rushed into the woods.

Others appeared outside—Jaguar, Jeshickah, Taro, Varick, more shapeshifter guards—and the fight began in earnest. I turned toward the woods, intending to hide the boy with the sakkri, who was least likely to actually engage in bloodshed.

I never saw the blow coming. It hit me from behind, sending me stumbling forward as the world darkened. As far as I could tell, I never struck the ground.

CHAPTER 22

AISLINN HAD PASSED *the magical toxin on to the other slaves each day for a week through a few drops of blood in the communal stew. When she uttered the invocation Alejandra had taught her, the power rolled like thunder spreading from a bolt of lightning, and the riot began. The other slaves—and not a few of the shape- shifter guards—reeled against hallucinations and fought shadows, unable to understand even the trainers who waded among them to try to regain control.*

Many of them died there, necks broken, before anyone noticed the fire creeping in from the north wing.

When it reached them, the stench of smoke was acrid, cloy- ing. Flames powered by a mix of magics—falcon, Azteka, Shantel, Triste—flickered in a dramatic rainbow of colors. Tapestries, car- pets, and priceless wood carvings burned yellow-orange, but the granite and marble walls and floors burned vibrant green and silver blue, low licking flames that seemed almost harmless unless you came close enough to hear the way the air whistled into them and feel the way your flesh started to sear.

Human bodies, when the magical fire caught them, also burned in shades of red, yellow, and orange.

In the east wing, slaves who were not currently on duty were resting when the smoke first began to seep down the hall. They had heard the commotion from the south wing, but ignored it because it came with no orders. They had seen guards running back and forth through the halls, but that too was meaningless to them, since those guards shouted no commands.

Likewise, when the smoke became thick, none of them struggled. There were no windows, but it would not have occurred to these bred and broken slaves to open one even if there had been.

I didn't want to watch that. I struggled toward consciousness—

Sara spun as she sensed movement behind her, nearly too late, then pulled back as tamer flames than those that devoured the stone face of Midnight engulfed a shapeshifter who had been unlucky enough to side with his vampiric employers.

She recognized the power that had cast that fire. It seemed Lila had retained her witch magic when she had taken a vampire's blood.

"Are you all right?" the once-witch asked.

Sara nodded sharply, hardly able to face the black eyes gaz-

ing out of the face she had once known so well. She had called this woman Auntie Lila when she had been a child. She had called Lila's twin children, Rachel and Alexander, her cousins.

This wasn't the time or place, but she couldn't keep the words inside. "We thought you were dead," Sara accused. "Your line was declared extinct when you disappeared with your children. Are Rachel and Alexander with you? Did you make them what you are?"

The last words were uttered with horror and disgust, emotions she saw mirrored on Lila's face, as if that possibility were just as obscene to her as it was to Sara.

There was no time to continue the conversation as the vampires began to arrive.

Alejandra flung a coil of magic at Jaguar, who collapsed like falling leaves, but that still left the other trainers. Lila turned to contain Taro, and Sara saw an opportunity to go for Jeshickah. The Mistress of Midnight was stalking the woods, looking for the source of the magic raining down on her empire, and hadn't noticed the hunter with a blade raised behind her.

She had her arm lifted to land the killing blow when the sakkri's prophecy came to her mind: "Sacrifice is not failure. All hesitation is not in vain."

Remembering what Nathaniel had said about vengeance, and how killing this creature would endanger all witches, Sara paused a heartbeat before she could have destroyed the creature responsible for this empire. In that time, Jeshickah sensed the danger and spun to defend herself.

There had to be a way out—

There was a point shortly before dawn when the fighting seemed to pause, like a wave receding. The world seemed to take a breath. Midnight's allies looked around and realized it was over.

Shevaun was the first of Nathaniel's group to step forward. The blood on her hands belonged to the slaves she had killed, and the ash on her skin was residue from burning Jeshickah's personal home to the ground, but Theron didn't need to know that. He assumed she had been on his side all along as she encouraged him to move on. They disappeared together.

Seeing the momentary pause, Alejandra dropped the bow she had been using and risked stepping out of her magical concealment. She threw Jaguar's arm over her shoulder, and bent her back to carry the semiconscious vampire away.

Nathaniel clasped Taro's hand to help him stand, and pointed out that Varick had already gone. It was time to find safer ground.

I struggled to open my eyes, which felt gummy, as if someone had glued them shut while I slept. I lifted a hand, which felt as heavy as the stones of Midnight itself, and wiped tarry fluid from my face.

Blood. Thick, half-dried blood, probably from the body that lay across my own.

As I fought to get out from under the dead shapeshifter on top of me, I discovered a knife still lodged in my chest, under my collarbone. My swiftly healing flesh had tried to push it out, and it clattered away when I brushed at it, but the wound—and the blood I must have lost through it—explained why I had been unconscious so long and why I felt so exhausted—

Sunrise.

The fact hit me like a blow, and I pushed myself up so quickly that I retched and the world spun. I fell back to my knees, gagging, as I took in the scene around me.

Only one pair was still fighting, but it wasn't us against Midnight anymore. Jeshickah had thrown Gabriel up against a tree and was accusing him of being involved in the attack. I saw her bury a dagger in his chest, close enough to the heart she probably meant to kill him before someone else grabbed her wrist, shouting, "Jeshickah, think! He wasn't behind this. His prizes burned, too."

His prizes burned, too.

Ashley.

Hara.

Alasdair.

I hadn't saved them. I had let them burn.

The horror that washed over me was almost enough to numb my recognition of the woman who dared to seize Jeshickah's arms, pulling her away from Gabriel before she slaughtered the trainer. She had thrown back the hood of the cloak that concealed her identity when she stood with the rest of us.

Now, every line of her face was familiar, and eerily similar to Jeshickah's.

Our employer, the woman who as far as I could tell had instigated, funded, and emboldened the fall of Jeshickah's empire . . . was Jeshickah's own sister, Katama.

And if she sees you looking, she will probably kill you to keep you from ever speaking, my common sense warned me. I didn't know why Katama had chosen this course, but she had been careful to keep anyone else from knowing her role.

But what was the point of going on now anyway? I had failed.

Not a single granite wall of Midnight remained. The molten slag, glowing white-hot, had nearly reached my prone form. If it had touched me, I would have had an instant funeral pyre. Had the boy survived, I wondered, or had he burned despite all I had lost trying to save him?

I was tempted to reach for the fire. To join Ashley, and all the other slaves I had consigned to death. If it hadn't been for Farrell, I would have died there years ago. Why not now?

Because Kadee and Vance are waiting for you, you fool.

It sounded like the sakkri's voice, but I saw no sign of her, and I didn't dare risk drawing attention to myself by trying to stand again until Gabriel, Jeshickah, and Katama disappeared.

When I tried to shapeshift, nothing happened. Between the magic I expended the day before and the blood I lost, my body was too battered for me to complete the change, so I stumbled into the woods instead.

I found Sara sprawled on the ground, her neck at an impossible angle. There were several shapeshifter bodies in the regalia of Midnight's guards, as well, but the witch was the only one of *us* I found left on the battlefield.

I had no supplies, and no way to get any. My clothes were plastered to my skin with blood and ash, and my only weapon was the knife I had pulled out of my own body. Nevertheless, I began the laborious walk toward the edge of Shantel land, stopping only briefly to drink my fill at a cold, babbling stream.

By the time I made it to the rendezvous spot, it was late afternoon, long past the hour when we were supposed to meet. The remnants of a campfire, now cold, greeted me. I felt utterly isolated before I spied a figure leaning against a tree, his eyes closed and chest rising and falling with the gentle rhythms of sleep.

I paused a moment, watching Vance sleep. He alone, it seemed, had waited. Had he known I would come? Hoped? Or just hadn't known what else to do? Kadee was probably still busy at the Shantel fleshwitch's hut, tending to the wounded, but Vance hadn't had a task to complete after the fire started.

Gently, I shook him awake.

At first, he gave no response except to blink his eyes as

if he were struggling to bring them into focus. Then, when he recognized me, he threw himself forward and wrapped his arms around me.

"They said you were dead," he said.

"It's easy to make that mistake about a white viper," I said, trying for a lighthearted tone, but failing. "Did . . . did anyone else make it out?"

Vance's gaze dropped, and he shook his head. "Nathaniel waited for hours for Aislinn. He said she had insisted on trying to save Hara, and that might delay her . . . but she never came. Kral says the fire spread to the back quicker than we anticipated. A couple of guards tried to get out that way, but then the tunnel collapsed, and no one else . . ." He trailed off. "I guess Gabriel tried to get back in, but the entrance was already blocked."

I nodded absently. Vampires normally had the ability to just blink out of place and appear elsewhere, but Jeshickah liked to control people coming into her domain, so she had witches design spells to make it impossible to come into Midnight that way.

His prizes burned, too.

"He was trying to save . . . Ashley," I said. To Gabriel, anyway, she was Ashley.

"The sakkri says he loves her."

I made a strangled sound, half laugh, half scream. What Gabriel thought he felt was probably what had saved

266

Alasdair from complete annihilation, but a trainer wasn't capable of love, not really. He never could have done the things he did to her if he had been.

"Kadee is all right?" I confirmed, though I was already sure. Vance wouldn't have been talking about trainers and slaves if anything had happened to her.

"She's helping the Shantel," Vance said. "They're . . . The sakkri never came to the rendezvous either. Only Nathaniel, that falcon girl Keyi, and I showed up."

The sakkri must have been lost, or else she would have returned, but I doubted everyone else was dead. Most likely, they had decided they didn't need or want to meet again. I knew Alejandra had taken Jaguar, and Shevaun had gone with Theron. Even if our arrangement had mostly been for mutual convenience, I was glad he had someone with him in the aftermath.

What of the others? Had Averill survived to take this story back to her kin? Would Lila live to see her children again? Was Silver's line already consolidating his empire?

My head spun.

"Sit down," Vance warned me. "You're so pale you're practically blue. Are you hurt? I should have asked earlier."

I sat and let Vance take care of me. He helped me strip off my blood-encrusted shirt so he could make sure I didn't have any other wounds, and refused to let me walk anywhere until he had rekindled the fire and served me the reheated remains of stew the others had made and eaten hours earlier.

I smiled as I tasted it. "Squirrel," I said.

Vance looked at me quizzically for a moment, and then he laughed. The first meal we had ever shared had been squirrel stew.

"I'm ready," I said, once I had eaten my fill and felt a little stronger. "We should let Kadee know we're alive, and then decide what to do next."

Please don't leave me, I thought. Vance and Kadee had other options. *Better* options, probably, than I could offer them—especially if Midnight was really gone. How selfish would I have to be, to encourage them to remain together in the shattered remnants of what had once been the Obsidian guild?

As selfish as I was when I spoke my prophecy a little over two decades ago: *Someday, my sister, you will be queen . . . and this place, this Midnight, will burn to ash.*

It had been a lie then. I had made it true. *Is that enough to let you rest in peace, Farrell? You gave up everything and dedicated your life to this task. I did it for you.*

I paused at the edge of the Shantel Family Courtyard as the truth crashed down on me. Past that wall was a civilization, a king and two princes. They were probably panicked about their lost witch, but they would also be celebrating. They were free, but I wasn't. I had never been free. I still had sins for which I needed to atone.

"I need to go to the serpiente," I told Vance.

"You need a few days of good food and deep sleep," Vance argued. "After that, if you want to go fight Misha, Kadee and I will go with you. Until then, Obsidian or not, I won't let you go anywhere."

I quirked a smile. A child of Obsidian didn't need or give permission, and Vance knew that.

Very well. I would stay a day, long enough to rest and heal. Then I would move on.

I didn't want to go anywhere near the royal or even public areas of Shantel land, but I made use of their resources in order to bathe and eat, and accepted the clothing they gave me to replace my own ruined garments, as well as a sleeping roll and blanket, which I spread in front of my campfire.

I lay down alone, but it wasn't long before Kadee and Vance joined me, guarding my back and sharing their warmth.

If only their presence could keep the nightmares away.

Over and over again, I watched Alasdair's golden feathers falling to the ground: the trainer, shearing her flight feathers on one of her first days in Midnight.

When it wasn't feathers, it was scenes from a serpiente royal bedroom. The rapid patter of feet, the shouting of guards, and a canister of oil and flame flew in an arc through the air. It shattered against the base of the bed, igniting the linens and canopy immediately.

Three-year-old Hara screamed.

She kept screaming, older now, as fire closed in on her from all sides.

Golden feathers. Black scales.

It all ended in fire.

When I woke, I first thought my face was damp from morning dew. Only as I blinked the sleep from my eyes did I realize I had been crying. I instinctively wiped the tears away before anyone could see them, then took a minute to marvel at the way my eyes felt swollen and I could taste salt on my tongue.

Like the ocean.

I had never seen the ocean. That was Gabriel's thought.

I knew Vance wanted us to take more time to rest, but it was time to see my sister and Farrell's son.

CHAPTER 23

MISHA WOKE WITH *a quiet gasp and a shudder, recoiling from the man in bed with her. In his sleep, Aaron instinctively tried to pull her back, but she shoved him away again. He grunted and rolled over, dragging the edge of the blanket to his chest as if he couldn't stand not having something to hold.*

She refused to think about what had disturbed her rest. These days, her dreams were always full of icy marble, black eyes, a smooth tormenting voice, and pain. It was bad enough waking from them when she was alone. After one of those nightmares, Aaron's arms felt suffocating.

She had to steel her courage before leaving the royal bed-chamber and stepping into the halls of the serpiente palace, reminding herself that no one would dare accost her now, or ever again. She was queen.

One of the guards outside the bedchamber shadowed her

silently as she walked in long strides, trying to look as if she had a destination instead of as if she were fleeing her mate.

Most of the Obsidian guild had claimed an area called the Opal Hall, which was adorned much like a small dancers' nest. As Misha paused in the doorway, Aika looked up from where she had been dozing, her swelling belly making rest increasingly difficult. It was also making both her and Torquil increasingly protective and therefore problematic. Once the babe was born, Misha suspected she would need to find a way to take them more firmly in hand.

Discreetly, of course. They were well liked by the others, and people tended to have an irritating affection for newborns.

Despite what we were going toward, Vance and Kadee seemed as anxious to leave as I was. Though the Shantel mouthed words of gratitude and hospitality, their hollow, mourning gazes drove us out as surely as our duty to our next task drew us on.

We were still a half day's ride from the serpiente palace when I stopped short, sensing someone through the trees, moments before a man in the regalia of the palace guard stepped out and demanded, "Who goes there?"

Normally, I would have turned to run, but . . . something wasn't right.

This man didn't have the aura of a guard, and his uniform appeared battered, no longer crisp and vibrant black and navy.

Kadee and Vance drew weapons, but I didn't, even though the man facing me had a bow pulled.

My instincts were rewarded a moment later as the guard relaxed his hold on the bow and, inexplicably, started to laugh.

"Obsidian," he said, shaking his head. "Naturally."

"What's going on?" Vance asked warily. He held his knife loose by his side, taking my cue that it wasn't time to fight, but still concerned.

"I'm Quentin. If I'm not mistaken, you're Malachi, Kadee, and Vance Obsidian. I'm sure you're aware that *Naga* Misha has put you all on a list of individuals wanted for treason." The guard spat the word "Naga," the serpiente title for their queen, as if it was poison. Before I could decide whether or not those words were a threat, he added, "That's good. We could use someone with experience. If you need anything, our camp is through this way."

He turned his back on us and started to lead the way through the woods. Vance, Kadee, and I exchanged glances, but were too curious to resist following. Soon we found ourselves approaching a rough encampment.

We were challenged again as we drew near. Unlike the first guard, this woman had only a knife, which looked more like a kitchen implement than a weapon. She wasn't wearing a uniform.

"Are you crazy?" the woman hissed. "What are you doing, bringing them here?"

"Where else would I bring them?" Quentin answered. "They're allies."

It was certainly the first time a royal guard had looked at me, or any child of Obsidian, and thought "allies."

"I take it your group is fighting Misha?" I asked.

"Fighting may be too strong a word," he answered.

" 'Hiding from' would be more accurate," added the woman. "Surviving, if we can."

Barely surviving, I thought, as Vance, Kadee, and I toured the ramshackle camp. These were not people used to living in the woods. Many were dancers, used to the most luxurious accommodations the serpiente had to offer. Others were merchants, shepherds, or craftsmen. Only a few were guards.

"Misha and Aaron have the palace guards tightly under control," Quentin explained. He seemed to be tentatively in charge of the exiled group. "Anyone who speaks up disappears for a few days, and comes back more . . . tractable."

I winced, imagining the persuasion that caused that kind of change. Magic was probably involved, but based on what I had seen in the palace months ago, it was surely mixed with physical cruelty as well.

"There are about two dozen of us," Quentin said as my gaze raked the camp.

Their shelters were barely sufficient for summer or fall; they were probably already becoming uncomfortable at night, especially for individuals used to soft living. The camp supplies I could see were obviously scavenged or improvised, few of them appropriate for their current uses. The Obsidian guild had always lived rough, and I had known plenty of cold and hungry nights when supplies were scarce, but we had been better off than this because we knew what we were doing. These people would never make it through the winter without help.

"Our only safety comes in the fact that Misha isn't comfortable sending guards to hunt us," Quentin added. "I don't think she trusts them to come back."

That was good news. Misha's magic wasn't all-powerful; it was significantly weaker than mine, and I had never had the strength to conquer a civilization.

Vance was the first to ask, "Does she know yet—for that matter, do *you* all know—that Midnight is gone?"

Quentin just stared at us at first, as if waiting for Vance to continue. After a long silence, he said, "Do we know . . . *what?*"

As we began to speak, Quentin hushed us, and called the rest of his band over. My skin crawled as we stood in front of the crowd, many of whom were looking at us with much more suspicion and loathing than Quentin. He seemed to have quickly grasped the idea that "the enemy of my enemy is my friend," but the rest were not so swift to trust members of the guild they had been warned about for a generation.

We didn't explain what our roles had been in the attack, but we described the fire, and what we had seen of the aftermath: the sludge of molten stone, the still-smoldering embers, and the lingering stench of the dead.

"My understanding is that another group of vampires plans to step in and take control over their own kind," I said, "but they don't care about the shapeshifters. We're on our own now."

I expected to see relief and celebration, and there were moments of that . . . but many faces fell. Quentin was the one who finally articulated what many of the others were thinking.

"That means Misha did it," he said, with what sounded like dawning horror. "She promised to fight Midnight, and now it's fallen—"

"The timing is a *coincidence*," Vance snapped. "Misha can't take credit."

"But she will," Quentin replied, "and that will make it even harder to convince people to stand against her."

I shook my head. I hadn't ever considered a civilized rebellion where everyone rose up against a corrupt queen. A covert assassination was more likely to succeed.

A woman in the crowd whose name I didn't know spoke up next, asking, "What happened to Hara? A lot of people won't fight Misha because they see no choice. We could easily overturn a white viper if we had a cobra to take the throne."

I resisted the urge to look at Kadee and Vance, an expression that would have instantly and absolutely given away my guilt in the matter.

Kadee answered for me. "We tried to save her," she said, voice heavy with sorrow that I knew was more sincere than mine would have been. "She was in Midnight when the attack happened, and we tried to rescue her, but . . . we were too late."

I appreciated that she said *we*. She said it as if she believed that I would have kept my word and tried to rescue the cobra we had allowed Misha to sell, if I hadn't been knocked out.

Unfortunately, the woman raised her voice again. "That isn't what I meant," she said. "I mean, what *happened* to her—really? I know what our new royal house says. I want the truth."

Again, thankfully, Kadee spoke up. This time her voice was softer, less sure, but no less honest.

"Misha," she said. "She came up with the plan. We"— she gestured to herself, me, and Vance—"we tried to argue with her, and she turned on us. I would have saved Hara if I could have, but there was no way."

"We couldn't even go to Hara to warn her," Vance added. "We're children of Obsidian. She never would have let us speak, and if she had, she never would have believed anything we said."

I thanked the fates that I had such companions with

me—dear, sincere Kadee, and clever Vance, who could lie so smoothly and carefully. The crowd seemed mollified, at least.

"Where is Julian?" I asked. I had always hated the old king, but if the serpiente insisted on having a king before they would get rid of their false queen, he was the only one left who could fill the role.

"Murdered," Quentin answered. "A man from the Obsidian guild was arrested for it. Aaron and Misha had him publicly executed as a way of disavowing themselves from his actions."

I felt myself blanch in a way I hadn't previously. Misha had only been on the throne a few months, and she was already using us as scapegoats. Was that how she planned to get rid of Torquil and Aika when they became too inconvenient?

"Who?" I asked, imagining my scattered kin. Even though many had followed Misha, I didn't have it in me to hate any of them.

"A mamba named Phillip," Quentin answered.

There was no one in our guild by that name. Asking Quentin for more details only made it clear that the poor serpent hadn't been one of ours. What unfortunate wretch had Misha sacrificed to hide what I had no doubt was her own crime? And did it make it better or worse that she blamed Obsidian, but killed a stranger?

Kadee, Vance, and I stayed with the group. Where

else? We were all exiles, with nowhere else to go and only the most tenuous of goals.

More importantly, we stayed close to each other, and watched each other's backs, because there were plenty of whispers from people who weren't happy to see us. I didn't want Vance or Kadee to show up one morning with a slit throat.

Bit by bit, we helped make the camp livable, applying our knowledge of how to survive in the woods and make do with minimal supplies. The three of us hunted almost every day. Without consulting the rest of us, Kadee sneaked into the palace and found Aika and Torquil; even pregnant, Aika refused to flee danger, but instead helped smuggle us supplies, information, and occasional allies.

Bit by bit, we learned the true depth of our disastrous situation.

I had negotiated with Nathaniel to protect the central market and fields, but I hadn't accounted for the reckless acts of panic. The market had been sacked within hours of Midnight's end. Any wares left there had been stolen or destroyed. There were also fights in the bloodtraitors' village. The fall harvests had been haphazard, and many of the food supplies on which the shapeshifter nations depended were either hoarded by those who had them, or left to spoil when no one organized their harvest, packaging, and transport.

Trade, which should have been revitalized for the

serpiente once they were unafraid of Midnight's laws, remained stagnant. The Shantel disappeared into the woods again instead of supporting the others and sharing the supplies they had prepared. No one could reach them. As for the avians . . .

"What do you mean, *missing*?" I demanded.

Vance didn't flinch. "Exactly what I said," he replied flatly. "Rumors say the avians' queen Miriam and her only child, Stephen, are both gone. They went for a meeting with Misha and Aaron, and never returned."

Would Aaron and Misha have attacked the Tuuli Thea and her heir?

Why *wouldn't* they? Misha was mad, and Aaron was so deeply in her thrall he had no sense of his own.

"Misha is threatening to greet any avian demands with soldiers," Vance replied.

I let out a frustrated growl. Midnight had fallen, but Misha wasn't content. She needed an enemy to fight. She wouldn't hesitate to start a war.

"I don't know if this means anything," another serpent said, "but I just got back from checking the market, where I finally found one of the Shantel. They're in rough shape—their sakkri never returned from the attack on Midnight, and their magic is volatile because of it—but they haven't completely abandoned us. While we were talking, he mentioned rumors that a golden-haired woman was seen talking to Prince Lucas. I don't know why Miriam would be with the Shantel, but . . ."

He trailed off with a hopeless shrug, dropping his eyes.

My heart nearly stopped.

Golden-haired woman. There was a possibility it was Miriam, of course . . . but there was also a possibility it was *Alasdair*. Could she have made it out? If she had, and she had been injured, someone might have brought her to the Shantel for healing.

"I need to go," I whispered.

I threw myself into the air, taking to my second form so rapidly I barely even heard Vance's startled yelp of, "Malachi! Wait!"

I couldn't wait for him. Even if we were willing to leave Kadee alone—which neither of us would be—Vance's quetzal wings could never keep up with mine, and I couldn't stand to slow my pace. I needed to know. *Now.*

CHAPTER 24

KEYI KNELT AT *the sakkri's side as the elderly witch shuddered and coughed. "So much bloodshed," the sakkri said. "So much ash."*

"Are you all right?" the falcon asked.

The sakkri shook her head. "My magic was never meant to be used this way. Help me back to my land?" she pleaded.

Keyi tried, but when they reached the border between Midnight and the magical forest of the Shantel, the sakkri stumbled and fell within arm's reach of her homeland.

"Oh, my sister," the sakkri whispered as softly as a prayer. "You were supposed to take this burden from me."

Keyi tried to help the sakkri stand, but the witch shook her off.

"No," she said. "It's over. This body is too old and too bloodied to hold such power anymore."

"Don't talk that way!" Keyi reached down to pull the sakkri to her feet with or without her consent.

But her work was in vain. Keyi's hands passed through the sakkri's dark skin as if it were nothing but a shadow . . . and then that's all that it was, an irregularly shaped shadow cast by the trees . . . and then even less than that. She was gone.

As soon as I passed above the Shantel forest, the world around me spun, driving me to the ground so hard it knocked the breath out of my lungs. I hit the cool earth and for several moments just lay there, trying to pull air into my body.

No, not just cool—*cold*. It was mid-October, but the ground already felt as frozen as the night Shkei had died, when I first met Vance. The land was mourning the sakkri.

I stood cautiously, wary of other magical traps. The air around me had a quiet, waiting feel to it. Would a new sakkri be born? Who would teach her to use her power?

I started walking, trying to guide myself by the magic around me, but I had only come to the Shantel woods guided by Nathaniel's tokens. I could only hope I would end up at the central village. If Alasdair was alive, that's where she would be.

If they haven't executed her, my cynical, despairing mind whispered to me. The Shantel didn't believe anyone who had been imprisoned in Midnight could ever be trusted again.

Night fell around me, but I trudged on, tripping over brambles and downed tree limbs. The woods showed damage as if from a fierce and violent storm, more extreme than anything we had actually experienced. Were they *dying*? Had the sakkri really sacrificed everything—not just herself, but her land and her people—in order to fight Midnight?

I had given everything *I* had as well, but an outlaw who refused responsibility for anyone or anything beyond himself could never have as much to lose.

By the time I reached the stone walls that ringed the Shantel village, I was trembling with exhaustion. My vision was swimming with ghosts of both the past and the future, bloody and wailing specters I couldn't quite vanquish. It was almost a relief when the guards appeared around me and grabbed my arms.

"Alasdair?" I said.

No one answered. I hadn't really expected them to. They hoisted me up and dragged me forward. I was grateful for the assistance; I couldn't walk anymore.

They didn't bring me to Alasdair. They didn't even bring me to one of the Shantel royals.

Instead, they brought me into a guest suite in the royal family's home, and dumped me in front of a woman with pale skin, ebony-black hair, and garnet eyes. How had she made it past the flames and out of Midnight?

"He's one of your people," I heard them say. "What would you like done with him?"

Hara Kiesha Cobriana stared at me, at first with confusion, and then with growing fury.

"Before you answer," another voice interjected, "you should know that Malachi was critical in the attack against Midnight."

I turned toward Lucas, grateful that he had come to my defense. The ruling prince had dark circles under his eyes.

"I've also heard that Misha and Aaron have declared him a traitor, and put a bounty on his head. It might be worth hearing what he has to say."

The magical pressures that had battered me on my way here had left me exhausted mentally and magically. I had little time left before my own power would force me into the dark void, where I would dwell until my body had recovered sufficiently for my mind to inhabit it. I needed to explain my presence. I needed to justify what I had done. I needed to convince Hara not to kill me out of hand, as I could see in her eyes she wanted to.

"Alasdair?" I croaked. My throat was tight, parched as if by the fires that had consumed Midnight. "Kill me if you want to, but please tell me first, did Alasdair survive?"

Hara's eyes widened, and then narrowed in suspicion. "Why do you want to know?" she asked.

If the answer was no, she would have said no. She knew the part we played in selling Alasdair. She would have blamed me for the hawk's death, if she could.

She's alive.

Darkness swallowed me.

"We need to go!" Aislinn shouted desperately. *Ever since she had triggered the spell, her skin had been tingling, and her muscles were heavy as if she had worked them to exhaustion. Now her eyes stung and her lungs burned from the smoke she had already inhaled—but that was nothing compared to what would happen if the fire reached them.*

Hara turned and gripped Ashley's hands. "I won't go without you. I never would have survived here all this time if you hadn't helped me. Please."

Ashley shook her head, her eyes wide and panicked. "I can't."

Hara wouldn't leave without Ashley, and they were running out of time. Knowing the mind of a slave better than anyone, Aislinn snapped, "Would he want you to stay here to die?" *The hawk gasped at the blunt words, but she started to move.*

Once in the halls, it seemed every way they turned was blocked. They couldn't get to the passage out. Even when they managed to find their way into the courtyard, the heat was so terrible Aislinn's skin had started to blister, and her head spun as she took in lungfuls of black smoke instead of clean air.

She was on the verge of unconsciousness when she saw Ashley look up at the sky, then shut her eyes with an expression of desperate concentration. The last image Aislinn saw was the pair of wide golden wings growing from Gabriel's slave's back.

I woke, unsurprisingly, in another cell.

I was getting to be quite a connoisseur of prisons. This one wasn't nearly as nice as Midnight's now-molten marble trainers' cells, or anywhere near as vile as the blood-stained hole Misha had thrown me in. It was simple, dry, and clean, with an earthen floor covered by a woven mat, a mattress, and a cubby set well away from the sleeping area with a basin for waste. There were no windows in the walls, but there was one—set with bars—in the heavy wooden door.

I debated breaking out, but in Shantel land, that seemed unwise. Instead, I approached the door and called, "Hello?"

I expected a guard.

Instead, another barred door diagonal to my own swung open, revealing a lithe, golden woman in a simple woolen dress.

She approached cautiously, her bare feet soundless on the dirt floor. When she pulled on the door to my cell, it opened without protest. It had never occurred to me that it might not be locked.

I opened my mouth, but couldn't find a single word. I wanted to cry. I wanted to beg her forgiveness for everything—for selling her, for not saving her, for leaving her to the fire. I wanted to thank her for everything she had done for my brother. I wanted to weep for her, for everything I had experienced with her in the trainer's cell.

I had been raised to hate every example of royal blood, but she had shown me what a queen should be, and *could* be: brave, wise, and compassionate. She had taught me that there were people who were worth following.

I couldn't speak, so I let my body speak for me: I went to my knees. As a child of Obsidian I bowed to no master . . . but as a child of Obsidian, I also had the right to choose my own path. This woman had earned my loyalty. Alasdair didn't pull away when I took her hand, silently pledging her everything. My faith, my love.

"My queen," I whispered.

She shook her head.

"Are you all right?" I tensed at the cold, protective voice I heard behind us. Hara hadn't had me killed in my sleep, but her tone suggested she wished she had.

Alasdair nodded, though I felt the slow shudder that passed through her. I remembered the time Jaguar had asked her the same thing. She had lied for me then, protecting me.

Now she protected me again. "I am fine," she said to Hara, her musical voice making the words echo in my head. "He wouldn't hurt me."

Fine.

Fine.

Everything will be okay now.

I looked up at Alasdair and Hara . . . and suddenly, I couldn't help but laugh, because I knew what came next. Hara had every right to hate me, given what my guild had done to her mother, father, and brother, all on the basis of my prophecy. I doubted she really wanted my help, but I needed to make that right somehow. And Alasdair *should* hate me, but somehow didn't.

Either way, there was only one thing left for me to do.

I, Malachi Obsidian, creation of Mistress Jeshickah, prophet and inspiration of the Obsidian guild, who had conspired against the greatest empires in the world, now had a goal: I would see not just one but *two* queens to their rightful thrones, or I would die trying.

EPILOGUE

THE WINTER WINDS *are bitter tonight. I had forgotten how frigid and biting the air can be outside the protection of Midnight's stone walls. This shelter is as comfortable as a structure made of wood and leather can be, but the howling wind makes the walls flutter and my bones tremble.*

I stare at the notes in front of me, trying to make sense of them. One of the few things that Hara and Malachi agree on is the fact that I cannot ignore the world. It is hard for me to believe that anyone truly needs me, but they keep insisting. So I read reports about food scarcity, riots, and how the serpiente and avian armies continue to grow as they struggle to contain their own people, and turn wary eyes to each other. I know that the Shantel have refused to see anyone since the day we left—even Kadee gets turned away when she tries to enter their forest—

and the Azteka have not returned to the marketplace since the equinox. Malachi says he suspects the sakkri knew she would not return from the attack, but also that they could not succeed without her.

Hara rails that I must attend to these messages, because it is my right and my responsibility to return to the avian people as monarch.

Malachi calls me his queen, but would let me be anything I want.

He would let me do anything I desire, would follow me into court intrigues or into exile. When, in an hour of weakness and desperation, I took my hawk's form and sought the small port town where I first met Gabriel Donovan, Malachi did not stop me. He followed, and his blue eyes watched without judgment as a half dozen different people told me that no one had seen Gabriel for months. When I came home to camp, he let me sit silently, mourning a man I know I should hate with every fiber of my being. And when I was ready, he put his arms around me, and I wished I could remember how to cry.

The only person who better understands how difficult it is to go through each day, needing to make the decision for myself to get up, dress, and put one foot in front of the other, is Aislinn. I didn't think she would survive the injuries she took from smoke and fire in our escape. By the time she had recovered enough to tell us anything, it was far too late for us to find Nathaniel, and we have no way of contacting him now. None of us have heard anything from the vampires; Silver's line has kept to their word to leave the shapeshifters alone. So Aislinn, too, will have to learn what it means to live without a master.

Privately I wonder how things might have been different if Nathaniel had gone to Gabriel to enlist his support. Gabriel worked hard to make sure that no one saw the cracks in his façade as a perfect, ruthless trainer, endlessly content with his brutal work. I do not think he knows how to be anything else, but sometimes I think he wanted to be. I don't think he would have actively assisted Nathaniel, but I think he would have walked away and let the winds blow where they would.

He would have taken me with him.

I know that thought should terrify me. Some days, when I can pull myself from the fog, it does.

Hara plans to move against Aaron and Misha soon. Malachi says his guild is behind her, even those who currently live in the palace. We haven't been able to find any sign of Miriam or her son, though one of the other Obsidian serpents says they think Misha may have had my sister killed when she refused to condone the new serpiente queen's plan. Hara has made me promise that, when she returns to the throne, so will I.

I have no desire for the avian crown, but I will do what must be done. How could I do any less, when I look around me and know the sacrifices that each member of our band has made in their effort to usher in a better world?

Life is not easy, but as the Obsidian guild says, a life lived in hardship and freedom is better than one lived in comfort and captivity. I have been a younger princess, raised in luxury, with *minimal responsibilities and little common sense. I have been a captive songbird, held in a cage by a man I believe wanted me because I reminded him of something he lost long ago, something he did not know how to hold without destroying.*

Can I be a queen?

Can I be Alasdair?

Can I be responsible for myself, answerable to my own conscience, as I step forward and try to lead?

I look around, and know I am not alone in wondering. We are all starting new lives now. We are all learning, through hardship and determination, what it means to be . . .

Free.

Alasdair Shardae
December 1804

ABOUT THE AUTHOR

AMELIA ATWATER-RHODES wrote her first novel, *In the Forests of the Night,* when she was thirteen. Other books in the Den of Shadows series are *Demon in My View, Shattered Mirror, Midnight Predator, Persistence of Memory, Token of Darkness, All Just Glass, Poison Tree,* and *Promises to Keep.* She has also published the five-volume series The Kiesha'ra: *Hawksong,* a *School Library Journal* Best Book of the Year and a *VOYA* Best Science Fiction, Fantasy, and Horror Selection; *Snakecharm; Falcondance; Wolfcry,* an IRA-CBC Young Adults' Choice; and *Wyvernhail.* Her most recent novels are the Maeve'ra trilogy: *Bloodwitch, Bloodkin,* and *Bloodtraitor.* Visit her online at AmeliaAtwaterRhodes.com.